EPIC

HISTORIC ADVENTURES

The Boy
and the Spy

The Boy
and the Spy

Felice Arena

Kane Miller
A DIVISION OF EDC PUBLISHING

First American Edition 2023
Kane Miller, A Division of EDC Publishing

Copyright © 2017 Felice Arena
Red Wolf Entertainment Pty Ltd

Page 154: Sicily Invaded by Allied Forces (1943, July 12) Townsville Daily
Bulletin, National Library of Australia nla.news-article 61838818
Cover images: Trevillion - MON66484 and MOK31439

For information contact:
Kane Miller, A Division of EDC Publishing
5402 S 122nd E Ave
Tulsa, OK 74146
www.kanemiller.com

Library of Congress Control Number: 2022934491

Printed and bound in the United States of America
1 2022

ISBN: 978-1-68464-537-4

For everyone who provided encouragement, feedback, advice and cups of coffee while I was writing this story – you know who you are! FA

il ragazzo
THE BOY

The boy is running as fast as he can.

And right behind him is a German soldier.

They charge through a flock of flapping pigeons.

"Halt! Halt!" the soldier bellows. He yells at the boy to stop, first in German, then Italian. "Did you hear me? Stop, or I will shoot!"

But the boy doesn't stop. In fact, he runs faster, his scuffed and well-worn shoes pounding hard on the cobblestones.

He smirks, remembering the picture he has drawn and stuck on the windshield of a German officer's jeep. It's a perfect sketch of the leaders of Germany and Italy – Adolf Hitler and Benito Mussolini – their faces attached to the bodies of plump pigs wallowing in mud and muck.

The boy turns down one of the side streets off the piazza. He charges to the bottom of the street, takes a sharp left . . . and smacks hard into an old fisherman carrying a bucket filled with sardines.

The tiny silver fish slide all over the ground, but the boy regains his balance and sidesteps the fisherman.

"*Disgraziato*! Wretched kid!" he hears the man shout.

He sprints on and glances over his shoulder. The soldier is slipping on the sardines and wet cobblestones and has toppled over the fisherman.

Safe, the boy thinks. Now I'll lose him!

He takes the coast road that leads out of town. There's no sign of the soldier. The boy slows to a jog, then a walk. The Mediterranean Sea shimmers in the early afternoon light – turquoise and serene.

But after a while he hears the distant echo of an engine.

A motorcycle appears over the ridge and comes speeding toward him. The boy shouts and takes off again. He veers off the road and heads toward the craggy seaside cliffs. Surely the soldier won't follow him there.

But the German soldier dumps his bike and

resumes the chase on foot. For a moment the boy questions his actions. Was a funny drawing worth being arrested for? Or shot?

In front of him is one of the highest cliffs in Sicily – the fishermen call it *il Diavolo*, the Devil. It has a curved ledge that protrudes over the surf. The men say it looks like the devil's horns. No one has ever jumped off *il Diavolo*. No one has ever been that stupid.

But now the boy has nowhere else to go. Could he jump? How could a twelve-year-old boy survive a forty-two-meter drop into the sea?

He remembers a time before the Germans arrived. He was only small, but he recalls when a professional cliff diver from Spain had come to dive off *il Diavolo*. The whole town was there – they all thought the diver was crazy.

The man had told them that the dive wasn't the hard part. It was the way you entered the surface of the sea. Enter it the wrong way, and you might as well be diving into solid rock. Do it properly and you'd be all right. But even the diver had chickened out at the last minute.

The boy slides to a dusty stop only meters from *il Diavolo*'s edge. He looks down and immediately feels dizzy and sick – deep-blue swells and rolling foamy waves crash up against the cliff wall far below him.

He takes a wobbly step back and waits for the soldier to reach him. On the ground in front of him he sees a silver pendant glinting in the sun. It's about the size of a thumbnail. He bends to pick it up and brushes off the dust – on it is an image of a saint and propped on the saint's shoulder is the baby Jesus. It's *San Cristoforo*, Saint Christopher.

The boy scoops it up and shoves it deep into his front pocket – for luck and protection.

The soldier is only meters away. He has fair skin, straw-like blond hair and blue eyes. For the first time the boy realizes he's not much older than he is. He looks too young to be in uniform.

"So you thought you could outrun me," the soldier says in heavily accented Italian. He pulls out his pistol from his belt. "You think you're so funny! You do realize that we are on the same side, don't you? Italy and Germany, the pact of steel. Unless you're a traitor and you want the enemy to win?"

The boy doesn't answer. His heart is thumping. There's nowhere to run except for a steep, narrow, craggy path that leads all the way down to the sea – but then what? Be shot as he tries to climb down? The boy decides to stay put and face his destiny, whatever that will be.

"Answer me!" says the soldier, raising his pistol and pointing it at the boy. "Don't make me shoot you." His voice is almost pleading. "All you have to do is say sorry, and we might let you go with a warning, *va bene*?"

The boy feels a flash of anger. Why should I say sorry when I'm not? And then he thinks of his mamma. What would it mean to her if he were caught? Even if they let him off. The boy sighs. He didn't think it through when he drew the picture.

This would surely put his mamma in danger, or at least put her under scrutiny by the Germans. They were already judged by everyone in town, seen as different from everyone else. How much worse would it be after he was marched back to town and accused of being a traitor? Was he really prepared to bring more shame on his mother?

The boy steals a glance over the edge of the cliff. Yep, it's a long way down.

"*Verstehst du mich? Capisci?* Do you understand me?" The soldier moves slowly toward him.

The boy is gripped by an intense, familiar feeling of frustration and impulsiveness. It washes over him.

He takes a deep breath, turns . . . and jumps.

la spia
THE SPY

The boy falls.

He remembers what the cliff diver said: "You must keep your body straight and stiff like a spear, and pierce the water with as little a splash as possible."

He tenses his body, glues his arms by his sides, and points his toes at the water . . . And harpoons through the surface of the sea.

A whooshing jet of bubbles envelopes him, making his skin tingle, his ears ring and his face vibrate. His heart feels as if it's been shoved up into his throat and his head begins to throb as he shoots downward toward the dark deep below.

His chest tightens. His vision blurs.

And then . . . there's nothing but blackness.

—

The boy blinks. At first everything is blurry, but things slowly begin to come into focus.

He sees a shadowy figure above him and immediately tries to scramble away.

A man's voice says something in a language that the boy doesn't know. It sounds a little like German, choppy and clipped. Could it be English?

"It's okay! Shhh!" the man says, now in Italian. "It's okay! I'm not going to hurt you. No need to panic." His voice is gentle. He's trying to be calming.

He's tall, taller than most of the men in the boy's town. He's not young, but not old either – he has flecks of gray through his mousy-colored hair and there's stubble on his chin. His eyes are marble gray and his expression is friendly.

The boy stops and looks around. He's in a sea cave, a grotto of some sort. The late-afternoon sunlight is streaming through the entrance. He doesn't answer the man. He's wondering whether to make a run for it or not.

"I don't know why I thought you'd understand

English," the man says. "Wishful thinking on my part, I guess. But we can communicate in Italian. And as long as you don't expect me to speak your Sicilian dialect, we'll be able understand each other. Okay?"

The boy nods warily.

He notices the man wincing as he crouches. His shirt is tightly wrapped around his left thigh – it's soaked in blood.

"So, kid," the man says. "I'm hoping you're not the son of a fascist or a Nazi, or I might as well kiss it all goodbye right now."

"Are you English?" the boy asks, finally mustering up some courage and allowing curiosity to get the better of him.

The man shakes his head. "No, I'm American," he says, pressing his hands against his injured leg and grimacing. "So, if you're not going to turn me in, do you think you might help me?"

The boy can't believe it, an actual American. His mother's best friend always talks about her cousins who moved to America years ago in search of a better life – but no one he knows has ever been there and come back.

"Why should I help you?" the boy asks. "You're *il nemico*, the enemy."

"That's a fair question. I'd ask the same if I were in your shoes."

There's a long pause.

"I'm asking you to help me because I saved your life," he replies softly.

The boy is taken aback.

"I'm a spy," the man adds bluntly. "But I guess you've already figured that out – why else would an American be in Italy? And because of this unexpected twist of circumstances, my life is now in your hands. So it's up to you to decide whether you owe me and will save *my* life. What's my fate? Are you going to turn me in?"

The boy sighs heavily and shakes his head.

The man exhales. "Thanks a lot, kid," he says. "I'm Christopher . . . Chris."

"You're called Cristoforo?" asks the boy, remembering the pendant in his pocket.

"Yeah, I suppose – that's how it's said in Italian."

"Here! A Cristoforo for Cristoforo," the boy says, handing it to him. "Keep it."

"Well, I'll take that as a sign of trust between us," says Chris, smiling. "And as Saint Christopher is the patron saint of travelers, I'll pray he helps me get out of this mess and gets me back home safely. So what's your name?"

"Antonio," the boy replies. "What happened to your leg?"

But before Chris can answer, Antonio shushes him.

From outside the entrance to the cave comes the sound of a motorboat.

la marea
THE TIDE

Antonio sits on the rocky ledge outside the entrance to the grotto watching a small patrol boat headed toward him.

He looks nervously behind him – the tide is coming in and soon the entrance to the grotto will be under water and hidden, but it's not rising fast enough. Soon Antonio will have to swim to get inside, but for now if anyone steps onto the rocky ledge that leads to the cave, they'll be able to wade right in.

Antonio squints at the boat, expecting to see the young German soldier. He takes a deep, nervous breath as the boat glides under the rocky cliff.

With relief he sees that the soldiers on the boat are

Italian, wearing tan-colored jackets with the usual two pleated breast pockets. Their trousers are tucked into their black boots.

"Hey, boy!" yells one of the two men on the boat, cutting the engine. "What are you doing down here?"

"I'm catching my breath," Antonio lies. But he has a plan. He's hoping to keep the soldiers distracted long enough for the tide to come in. The grotto will flood, but the water level won't reach the back of the sea cave, which slopes upward – Chris can retreat there, remaining safe and dry.

"Really?" says the other soldier, glaring at Antonio. "How did you get here? I don't see a boat."

"I don't have one," Antonio answers, looking up at *il Diavolo*. "I jumped. Could I catch a ride back to town with you?"

The two soldiers burst out laughing as if they've been told the funniest joke ever.

Antonio recognizes them. He's seen them around town – it's Vitti and Morelli. Vitti is tall and skinny, his slim face punctuated by a bushy unibrow. He seems out of place in his uniform. Morelli has an athletic build – broad shoulders and giant hands – and he looks every bit the soldier. He has a very fashionable moustache. Both look in their mid-twenties.

"Jump! Yeah, right. Nice try, *rota*," says Morelli.

Antonio tenses. Hearing the term *rota* is like getting a knife deep in his guts.

"I've seen him around town," Morelli says to Vitti. "Always roaming the alleys like a stray dog."

Antonio wishes they'd stop talking about him as if he's invisible and worthless.

He knows that the word *rota* will follow him his whole life. It means he was an unwanted baby, left in a wooden wheel attached to the wall of the local convent. Antonio was lucky – his Mamma Nina adopted him. But the town did not accept him as Nina's son. He would never be anything more than a *rota* to them.

"Move aside!" Morelli barks, preparing to jump off the boat into the shallows. "I'm going to have a look inside the cave."

"What are you looking for?" asks Antonio, blocking him.

"An enemy plane crashed off the coast a couple of nights ago and we're checking the area," says Vitti.

Morelli shoots Vitti an aggravated look. "The boy doesn't need to know that!" he says.

Antonio feigns excitement. "Were there any survivors? Was it English? Was it a Spitfire? Can I help you look for them?"

"No!" Morelli snaps. "Get out of the way."

"Well, don't waste your time. There's nothing in there," Antonio says. He knows he has to stall them a little longer.

He sighs. "I wish I'd been found by the Germans," he says. "I can't believe you guys won't give me a ride back to town. The Germans would've helped me. No wonder they think their army is better than ours."

"We're on the same side, *stupido!*" Morelli snorts.

"Yeah, but they still think they're better than us Italians . . . Maybe they're right. Maybe the *tedeschi* are just superior – and really can do everything better than us."

"Well, they're not better at soccer!" Vitti cuts in. "We're the best in the world!"

"Huh, soccer," Antonio says, pretending to consider it. "I hadn't thought of that."

"And food!" Morelli declares. "Our food is way better than the sour mush they eat."

"I suppose you're right." Antonio shrugs, noticing that the tide has now covered over half the entrance to the grotto. "Food and soccer – *viva Italia!*"

Morelli shakes his head. "Smart aleck," he hisses. "Let's go, Vitti! The tide's come in anyway."

"What about me?" Antonio asks. The sea is lapping up around his ankles, even on the ledge. "Come on – take me back to town!"

"If you really expect us to believe that you jumped off that cliff and survived, then you don't need our help – you can swim back!" Morelli shouts, as Vitti steers the boat away and motors back toward the shore.

As soon as the Italian soldiers disappear around the cliffs, Antonio dives into the sea and swims underwater through the entrance of the grotto.

"That was close," says Chris, as Antonio surfaces inside the cave. "I thought for sure that I was a goner. But it sounded as if you kept your cool out there. You know what, kid, you have the makings of a top spy. I think we'll make a great team."

Chris smiles, but Antonio is thrown by the compliment. Apart from Mamma Nina, he can't remember anyone saying anything kind to him before. He smiles back awkwardly, not sure how to react.

He's relieved when Chris asks about the path leading back up to the top of the cliff.

"Can you climb it?" he says. "I noticed it when I first made my way in here, but with this injury there's no way I can make it." He points to his injured leg. "I need your help, Antonio. Bandages, medical aid, food and water . . . whatever you can get your hands on. And I need to get out of here before the next patrol. You know they won't stop searching until they find something."

The American winces in pain again and Antonio takes this as his cue to go. He nods before he dives back into the water, but it seems like an impossible task – where on earth is he going to get medical supplies?

il quaderno
THE NOTEBOOK

"*Figlio mio!* My son! Is that you?" asks Mamma Nina.

"*Sì,*" Antonio bellows, slamming the front door.

Home is only three small rooms in a stone house in the center of town, but Antonio is grateful for it. He knows that without Mamma Nina, he'd be on the street or in an orphanage.

Mamma Nina is tossing fish in a bowl of flour in her tiny kitchen. More are frying on the stove. Antonio kisses her on the cheek, noticing her breathing is shallow.

"Dinner smells good," he says.

"Signor Piccolo is a good fisherman. And a good man, thank God. He's given us some of his catch again," she says. "Where have you been? And why are you soaking wet? Get yourself out of those clothes or you'll catch a cold."

Antonio moves to the corner of the living room where his bed stands. There's only one bedroom in this tiny house – and that's where Mamma Nina sleeps. Beside his bed is a set of drawers made from an old olive crate. He takes a white tank top and a pair of shorts out of one of the rickety drawers. He quickly changes into them and hangs his damp clothes on the headboard to dry.

"Signor Piccolo said he's going to Siracusa tomorrow to visit his sick sister," says Mamma Nina.

"Aha," mumbles Antonio, pulling out a notebook and some charcoal sticks from the bottom drawer.

"So we won't have fish until he gets back."

Antonio sighs, but he's not really paying attention. He opens his notebook to a blank page

"Maybe I'll make some *caponata* instead," Mamma Nina continues.

Antonio doesn't respond. He's concentrating on what he loves to do more than anything else – drawing. He sketches his day – the Saint Christopher pendant, a silhouetted figure jumping off *il Diavolo*, and a rough but true portrait of the American spy.

"*Allora, Antonio, mangiamo!* We eat!" says Mamma Nina, placing the fish and a loaf of bread on the table in the middle of the living room. Antonio puts his notebook back in the drawer and joins her.

He stabs hungrily at the fish with his fork.

"Ah! Ah!" snaps Mamma Nina, slapping his hand. "*Aspetta!* Wait! Let's pray. Dear God, we thank you for this meal, for Signor Piccolo, and for the good people in this world. We thank you for your protection and pray that this war will end soon. Bless us, and my *amore*, my love, Enzo, with you in heaven above. Amen."

Antonio looks up to the portrait of Enzo hanging on the wall by the front door. Mamma Nina prays before every meal. And in every prayer she mentions her late husband.

Too bad I didn't know you, thinks Antonio. It would've been nice to have a father. I'm sorry you died before Mamma Nina took me in. She loves and misses you very much.

The portrait of Enzo hangs next to the only other two paintings in the house. One is of Jesus. The other is of a farmhouse and a flock of sheep grazing in nearby fields – with a hillside town visible on the horizon. This was where Mamma Nina spent her childhood before she married Enzo and moved to the coastal town where she and Antonio live.

"Eat!" Mamma Nina says, opening her eyes.

Antonio digs in. He's famished.

"Slow down! You're going to choke."

Antonio stops for just a second and then continues to eat rapidly.

"Signora Lari told me that Signora Rocca's son, Filippo, has returned from living in Milano . . ." Mamma Nina always relates what she's overheard in town to Antonio.

He nods and continues to stuff his face. He rips into some hard, crusty bread and, while Mamma Nina launches into her story, stealthily shoves a piece of it into the pocket of his shorts – food for the American.

"Filippo has a wife, and a daughter about your age. The wife, I think, is from Switzerland – she has some kind of an accent. Or that's what Signora Lari told me anyway. I remember Filippo from when he was a boy. Enzo hired him to be his assistant one summer at the post office. He was very intelligent. They live in the top apartment in the building right next to the Santa Maria. You know the one? But you would hardly remember since you never go to church anymore . . ."

Antonio rolls his eyes.

"Anyway . . ." Mamma Nina continues. "Filippo is now a doctor. His mother must be so happy . . ."

"Wait! A doctor?" Antonio says. "As in, a doctor with medicine and bandages, doctor?"

"Of course," says Mamma Nina. "Are you sick?"

"Um, no, um – it's just good that we have someone like him around here. You know, for you," says Antonio.

"Now don't you worry about me," says Mamma Nina, standing up and taking Antonio's plate. "I'm feeling better today. Stronger than I've ever been."

But Antonio knows Mamma Nina is lying. She has been ill for a long time now. Every night he hears her coughing and wheezing in her room. And some days she has been too weak to get out of bed.

"Look what I have, a little treat tonight," she says, returning to the table with a small bowl of ripe figs. "From Signora Lari's cousin's farm. It's a little early in the season for them, but I'm not complaining." Mamma Nina smiles warmly. Antonio reaches for one of the figs, lost in thought.

He can't believe his luck. Food is rationed – they only get a little – but he knows he can save a piece of fruit or bread for the spy from his own share. Medical supplies, though, are much harder to find.

This is a godsend, he thinks. And if it's sent by God, then God won't mind me stealing it in this case, will he?

la chiesa
THE CHURCH

Antonio is lying in his bed, drawing in his notebook by the light of a lantern.

He is waiting for the right time to leave, when the town is dead quiet and everyone is fast asleep.

"Okay, this is it," he whispers, hopping out of bed. Antonio sneaks toward the front door but stops when he hears Mamma Nina coughing. It's a deep, raspy, barking cough. It doesn't sound good. He grabs a cup of water and takes it to her bedroom.

"Here, Mamma, have this," he whispers in the dark, lifting her head from the pillow. She sips at the water.

"*Grazie, figlio mio.*" She gasps and gulps for air,

then lays her head back on the pillow. The coughing has stopped for now.

Antonio leans over and gently kisses her on the forehead. "You're okay, now. Sleep well, Mamma," he whispers.

He closes Mamma Nina's bedroom door behind him and leaves the house. Antonio darts through the cobblestone streets, edging along the walls like a cat. He is nimble and quiet. When two German soldiers suddenly emerge from around a corner, he disappears into the shadows of an archway, waiting for them to pass.

Phew! That was close, he thinks, as their laughter fades in the distance.

Soon Antonio is standing in front of Dr. Filippo Rocca's home, next to the church, Santa Maria.

Antonio looks up to the top floor. One of the doors to the balcony is open.

Perfect, he thinks. Now all I have to do is get up on the roof and drop down onto the balcony. But how?

Antonio looks at the bell tower of the church.

"That's it," he says under his breath as he runs over to the heavy wooden doors of the Santa Maria.

He steps inside and is hit with the smell of centuries of dankness and incense. It's dark. It's cold. It's unnerving. Antonio looks up at the giant woodcarving of Jesus on a crucifix – it's as if he's looking disapprovingly at him.

The moonlight streams through the arched stained glass windows. Shadows flicker across large, ornately framed paintings hanging on the stone walls. Antonio shivers.

There's no denying it's spooky.

He sees a candlelight glow coming from the vestry at the side of the church. Could Father Dominic be in there now? Antonio inches toward the doorway and peeps in. There's no sign of the priest.

I suppose he would've heard me come in if he were here, Antonio tells himself. He turns back into the church and makes his way toward the bell tower.

The door to the tower is locked. As Antonio turns back toward the vestry to look for keys, he hears the creak of the front door opening – someone's coming into the church!

Antonio drops to the floor, crawls under the first two rows of the pews – and freezes.

He hears Father Dominic talking with another man, their voices getting louder as they walk up the center aisle, closer to where Antonio is hiding.

"I was just about to leave," Antonio hears Father Dominic say. "I didn't think you were coming, and a couple of soldiers came in earlier, wondering why I was here so late."

"This is where you're supposed to be, at any time of the day," says the other voice. "That is why this arrangement works so beautifully." To Antonio the voice sounds gruff and menacing.

As they move past him, Antonio catches a glimpse of the man with Father Dominic. Even in the shadows, he recognizes him – it's *La Vipera*, the Viper. Everyone in town knows him . . . or knows of him. He's a cold-blooded gangster – Antonio has seen his men in the piazza threatening business owners for money. No one messes with the Viper – not if they value their lives.

Antonio freezes, pressing himself down onto the church's tiled floor.

What's *he* doing here? What arrangement are they talking about? And why is he meeting with Father Dominic?

Father Dominic unlocks the door to the bell tower and enters. A few minutes later he returns with a cloth sack.

"Trust me. It's all there," he says, pulling out a fistful of money. "May the Lord forgive me for what I do and guide you back to redemption."

The Viper snatches the sack out of the priest's hands

and grabs the front of Father Dominic's cassock. "I don't need God's forgiveness, cousin," he snarls.

Antonio flinches. Did the Viper say *cousin*? He didn't know that the two men were related. He wonders if others in town know. Of course they do! he concludes. This is Sicily – everyone knows everyone's business, but everyone pretends to know nothing.

"All I need is for you to do what you're told . . . or people will get hurt," adds the Viper. "*Capisci*? Stick to what we've agreed."

The Viper releases his grip on the priest and leaves. Antonio notes Father Dominic's expression. He looks guilty. He looks distressed. He looks trapped. As the priest slowly makes his way toward the front doors, Antonio makes his move.

He dashes through the open door of the bell tower and runs up to the very top. He climbs onto the ledge where the bell hangs and without stopping to think, he fearlessly leaps out toward the roof of the building next door.

At first it feels just like it did when he jumped off *il Diavolo*, but below there is no water, no chance of survival, just the hard cobblestones of the street.

Thankfully, within seconds, Antonio feels the thud of his feet landing on the tiles of the gently sloped roof. He crouches down, his legs tensing and jarring at the impact – but overall it's a perfect jump.

He lies down on his stomach, crawls over to the edge, and hangs his head over the gutters. He can see the Viper walking away into the darkness.

"Okay, here goes," Antonio whispers. He hangs his legs over the ledge and gently drops a meter down onto the iron balcony.

Antonio takes a deep breath and steps through the open doorway. It takes a few seconds for his eyes to adjust to the darkness of the room. When they do, he realizes he's in a bedroom – someone is asleep in the bed on the other side.

Antonio sneaks toward the door. I'll check the bathroom and living room for the doctor's medicine bag, he thinks, and then I'll just leave through the front door and make a run for it . . .

But suddenly the room lights up. Antonio whirls around.

"Who are you?" A young girl is sitting up in bed, with her hand on the bedside light. "And what are you doing in my house?"

la ragazza
THE GIRL

Antonio edges toward the balcony.

The girl is oddly calm for someone who has been woken by an intruder. "Stay where you are," she says, "or I'll scream and wake my parents."

She steps out of bed – her voice is confident and strong and Antonio finds himself standing still even though every instinct in him is telling him to run.

"I mean it!" says the girl. "Who are you and what are you doing in my room? Are you here to rob us?"

Her face is porcelain smooth and her green eyes are almond shaped. Even in his panic, Antonio knows she's the prettiest girl he's ever seen. And even though she's caught him breaking into her house she doesn't have the judgmental expression he's used to seeing from other kids in his town.

"No," Antonio says. "I mean, not really."

He thinks about spinning some epic lie to explain why he's there, but this girl might still call the *polizia* or, even worse, her parents might drag him home and tell Mamma Nina.

And what would lying achieve? he thinks. The spy is counting on me – I need those supplies and there's no other way to get them.

Besides there's something about this girl, something real, something true. She really seems to want to know the answers to her questions and Antonio's instincts are telling him to be honest.

"Well, yes," he says finally. "But it's not what you think. I don't want money or anything to sell. Your father's a doctor and I need some first aid supplies . . . but I can't say why."

The girl suddenly turns her head toward the closed bedroom door. Antonio can hear footsteps approaching.

"Hide!" she whispers. She gestures for Antonio to crawl under her bed.

He does, just before the bedroom door swings open. He can see a woman's feet walking toward the bed.

"What are you doing up? I thought I heard you talking."

Antonio holds his breath.

"I can't sleep, Mamma," says the girl. "And I'm hungry."

Her mother sighs. "I told you you didn't eat enough tonight. I'll go get some pecorino and bread."

Then the girl says something Antonio can't understand. For the second time in a day, he hears the short clipped words of another language. But this time he recognizes it.

"No! No! What have I told you? No!" the mother snaps in Italian. "You can't speak English. Not even at home. Do you know what they would do to us if they discovered we speak the language of the enemy?"

"Sorry, Ma. I know," the girl replies. "It just slipped out."

Her mother leaves and she bends down to face Antonio under the bed, her hair hanging over her upside-down face.

"Just stay there for moment," she says. "My name's Simonetta. My mother will be right back. Tell me why you need first aid and maybe I can help. Are you sick? Hurt?"

"No," Antonio whispers. "But can you get me some supplies? If you do I promise not to tell the Germans you speak English." He grins. "I'm sure they'd be interested . . ."

The girl screws up her face, as if she's just been beaten in a game. Antonio snorts. Now they are even.

Simonetta's mother returns with a plate of cheese and bread and a few almonds.

When she says goodnight and leaves the room again, Antonio crawls out from under the bed. "So are you going to help me?" he says. "I need bandages and anything else you have that will help heal a wound."

"You can at least say please," says Simonetta.

"Pleeeease," says Antonio begrudgingly.

Simonetta straightens her nightdress and quietly sneaks out of the bedroom. A few minutes later she comes back in with a cloth sack, handing it to Antonio.

"There are bandages, iodine, Mercurochrome and aspirin in there. Hopefully they won't check for a while because my parents don't miss a thing. But, by then . . . well, I'll think of something to say. What's your name?"

"It's not important," Antonio says, pointing at the plate of food. "Can I have the cheese and bread too?"

He scoops up the food and drops it all into the sack.

Simonetta looks worried. "If someone is in

trouble – and it sounds as if someone is – then let me help," she says. "I know a lot about first aid. I've watched my parents for long enough. When your father's a doctor and your mother's a nurse, you pick up a few things."

Antonio sighs. As well as being confident, she's headstrong and persistent. "I don't want your help," he says, but seeing a disappointed look on her face he adds, "Sorry, but it's complicated. Now, how do I get out of here?"

Simonetta grins. "Didn't you just say you don't need my help? What was your plan? Break in here, grab what you wanted and walk out the front door?"

"Sounds good to me," says Antonio. "Can't I just do that?"

"My *nonno* and *nonna* sleep in the room next to the front door and unlocking it would wake them up," says Simonetta. "You really didn't think this through, did you?"

Antonio clenches his teeth. He hates to admit it, but she's right. He's always gone with impulse and instinct – but ever since he stuck that drawing on the German jeep, things haven't quite been working out.

"No, I didn't, Miss Know-it-all," he says.

"Relax. Don't lose your cool," she says. She starts pulling the sheets off her bed and grabs a couple more from a cupboard in the corner of the room – then ties them in knots to make a makeshift rope.

Simonetta waits for a German jeep to roll by and then throws one end off the balcony and hands Antonio the sack. "Don't slip," she says. "Whoever you are."

Antonio nods and climbs over the balcony. He slides down the bedsheet rope and as soon as he hits the ground, he can hear the sheets being pulled up over the balcony rail.

As he dashes off toward a side street, he looks back. He can't help hoping that Simonetta is still standing there waving . . . but the balcony is empty and the room is dark.

il complimento
THE COMPLIMENT

It's dawn and Antonio is up and moving again.

He squints into the morning sunlight as he makes his way out of town toward *il Diavolo*. In one hand he is carrying the sack filled with medical supplies, food, candles, and some water in a canvas bag – and in the other hand a fishing pole. He has no intention of fishing, but the Germans don't know that. As a couple of soldiers in a jeep drive past, they glare for a second, make an obvious assumption, and drive on.

It's a lot tougher climbing down the bumpy cliffside track than climbing up it. Antonio step-slides down the dusty narrow path that snakes down to the grotto, grasping on to rocks to keep his balance. He's glad he has left the fishing pole at the top – it's hard enough carrying the sack.

"Hello?" Antonio calls, when he reaches the bottom of the cliff. The tide is out and he can step into the grotto.

Before his eyes even have a chance to adjust, he's grabbed from behind, his mouth cupped by a coarse hand. His heart is pounding. He can feel the cold barrel of a pistol under his chin.

"Whoa, kid!" Chris exhales, releasing his grip on Antonio. "You just can't creep up on me like that!"

The American limps a few steps and falls to the ground, looking more exhausted than before. The morning light streaming through the entrance of the grotto is dim, and the interior of the cave is darker than the previous time Antonio was there.

He catches his breath, his gaze still on the gun. It's stamped and turned steel. It looks cold and deadly. He has never seen one like it before – it's nothing like what the Germans or Italians carry.

"It's the FP-45 Liberator," says Chris. "Single-shot action. And next time you need to give me some kind of signal. Maybe we should have a whistle."

The American whistles in three short pitches while uncocking the pistol.

"I hope there's something to eat in there," Chris

says, pointing to the sack in Antonio's hands. Antonio passes it over and the American rummages through it as if he's digging for treasure.

He shoves the bread into his mouth, and swigs down water. Antonio crouches beside him and separates the first aid supplies from the food.

"Whoa, kid. What did you do, rob a doctor or something?" Chris says with his mouth full, now grabbing for a fig.

"Yes," says Antonio matter-of-factly, lighting one of the candles he packed. He notices Chris is impressed.

"Nice work," Chris says. He begins peeling back his bloody shirt from around the top of his left leg.

Antonio winces when he catches sight of the wound. It's a gruesome, deep gash, surrounded by dark bruising.

"It's pretty nasty, eh?" Chris says, gritting his teeth. He begins gingerly cleaning the cut with iodine and applying the Mercurochrome. "Move the candle a little closer; I need to see what I'm doing here. And hand me the bandages."

Antonio does.

"There you go." Chris sighs heavily, wrapping the fresh clean gauze around his thigh tightly. "That should ward off any infection and I'll be up and running in no time. If I'm lucky and make it back home, I'll have a terrific story to tell."

"So what is your story?" asks Antonio.

"You mean my life story?"

Antonio nods.

Chris sighs. It's obvious that the American is reluctant to talk. But Antonio is curious, and is dying to know more about this man from the other side of the world.

"Come on – tell me. You know what it took me to get these medical supplies. What a risk it was."

"You're right, kid. If we're to trust each other . . . All right then, here goes. I'll give you a scaled-down version. I don't want to bore you."

Antonio grins, as the spy wriggles into a more comfortable position, wincing as he shifts his wounded leg.

"Only eight months ago I was a college professor," says Chris. "I used to teach Italian at Columbia University in New York – which is famous for its Italian department. Lorenzo Da Ponte taught there."

Antonio is confused. "Should I know him?" he asks. "Is he from around here?"

Chris laughs. "No, but he's one of your famous countrymen. He was the librettist for some of Mozart's most famous operas."

Antonio shrugs. "Who the prickly pear is Mozart?"

"Come on, you must know Mozart. The world-famous composer from the eighteenth century?

"Anyway, I taught there. And I know what you're thinking, how does an American end up teaching Italian? Two words: Marina Buonamici. She was my high school sweetheart – her parents had come to America from Genoa. And I wanted to impress her so much I taught myself Italian. Marina and I didn't last, but I discovered I had a talent for learning languages so I majored in Italian in college and before long I was teaching it."

"How did you become a spy?" Antonio feels impatient. He's waiting for Chris to get to the best bits of the story.

"I was approached by a US intelligence agency called the OSS, the Office of Strategic Services. They were searching for anyone who could speak and understand the language of our enemies, that is, Italian or German."

"I got that part," Antonio says. "I guess we're the bad guys in your story."

Chris nods and looks apologetic. "Yeah, well, anyone who speaks the language and is fit and prepared to serve their country makes a perfect candidate to become an operative for the agency. My wife's father fought and was killed in the First World War, and in her eyes he was a hero. So when the OSS came knocking on my door, I thought, here's my chance to do my part. They enlisted me immediately. Fast-forward several months later and I'm in a camp in North Africa training in combat warfare and code breaking. And only a couple of days ago I set out on my first mission . . . on a flight to Northern Italy."

"Wait!" Antonio says. "This is . . . was your first mission?"

"Yeah, not a great start, right? I was part of a six-man team and we were forced to bail out of the plane over the southeastern coast of Sicily. There was a fierce storm. I was lucky to get out before the aircraft crashed into the sea. I don't know about the others." Chris pauses. He gazes off to the side, and his entire body seems to deflate. "I might be the only survivor."

"And?" says Antonio, softly. "How did you get here?"

"I thought I would die," Chris says, his voice cracking. "My parachute opened, but I was blown miles away from the crash site – whipped about in the storm like a stringless kite. Then the wind tossed me against these cliffs – my leg took most of the force of the impact. Somehow I was able to get to my feet, sink my parachute in the sea and hide out in here."

Chris sighs. "Anyway," he says, suddenly shifting the mood. "That's my story. So far." He pulls something from the sack. "What's this?"

It's Antonio's book of drawings.

"Um, that's not for you. It's mine, sorry," says Antonio, snatching it back. "I, um, I just put it in there because I'm used to taking it with me wherever I go. It's nothing. I just like to sketch in it."

"Can I have a look?" Chris asks, extending his hand.

Antonio has never shared his drawings with anyone except for Mamma Nina, and even then, only rarely.

"Come on. Please?" the American says.

Antonio reluctantly hands over his notebook. He is nervous and slightly embarrassed. He watches Chris slowly and intently turning through the pages. Antonio is trying to read his expression. Chris is not giving much away. But then halfway through the book he looks up at him and smiles.

"Wow, kid, wow! You have talent. These drawings are fantastic! So you're an artist. Is that me?" Chris points at the illustration Antonio had drawn the night before. "You did my portrait! It's really me. And who's this woman? Is that your grandmother?"

"No, that's my . . . um, mother."

"What's with the pause? You're not sure whether she's your mother or not?"

"No, she's my mother. It's just that . . . um, it doesn't matter."

"Oh, okay. What about your dad?"

"I don't have one."

"Brothers or sisters?"

"No," Antonio says bluntly.

"Just you and your mom?"

Antonio nods.

"Well, I'm a dad. I live with my wife, Betty, and my daughter, Rose. She's six years old." Chris looks away, flipping through the notebook again. "They'll be so worried about me."

Again there's silence.

"Your sketches of buildings and the streets of your town are so realistic. You have a real gift, kid. And it's given me an idea. But first things first." Chris's voice is serious now. "I need to somehow communicate with headquarters and report my status. I'll have to arrange for rescue. I need to make contact with the *partigiani*, the partisans, or least that's what they're called in the north of Italy. They're sometimes known as *la Resistenza*, the Resistance. But down here I'm not so sure."

"*Partigiani*? *Resistenza*?" Antonio repeats. These are words he hasn't heard before.

"Yes. Locals who are against the Nazis and the fascists and are secretly helping the British and the Americans – the Allies."

"You mean like me?" Antonio asks. "I must be a *partigiano* because I'm helping you."

Chris chuckles. "Yeah. I suppose. Yes, you are. But I need groups of people. People who are against what Hitler and Mussolini stand for – against the dictatorship. And I'll need you to be my eyes and ears . . ." He looks down at his wound. "And legs, for now, at least. Intelligence has told us that there's an underground movement slowly building here in the south, but it's incredibly small, hidden, and it's difficult to pinpoint the players involved. Kid, this isn't a game. This is deadly work, and if you reveal yourself to the wrong people, I don't know what will happen . . . I'm sorry to involve you, but you're my only hope of getting out of here."

Antonio's mind races. Life has been tough since the Germans moved in – despite what some people said. Most people in town loved the Prime Minister of Italy, Benito Mussolini. And many of them also talked well of the Chancellor of Germany, Adolf Hitler. But Antonio hated the things that had happened since they joined

Germany in the war.

All my life I've been made to feel different or second rate because I'm a *rota*, he thinks. Supporters of Mussolini and Hitler treat everyone that way – like they're better than everyone else, like they should control the world. They say things like "we're born to fight" and "no one can challenge us."

"Why can't people just get on? Why do they have to judge other people?" he asks Chris.

Chris shakes his head. "I don't know," he says. "But it sounds like you know what it's like not to be given the freedom to be who you are. The Nazis don't treat people justly and humanly. They want to take away our basic human rights and liberties."

Antonio nods. "I can do this," he says intently. "I know how to be invisible. No one looks at me anyway. I'm just a *rota* – a ghost to most people. What do I need to do?"

"A *rota*?" says Chris. "That means a wheel. What do you mean you're a wheel?"

Antonio takes a deep breath and explains what it means. He looks to see if Chris's expression changes. Is he disappointed? Disgusted? Will Chris still want his help once he finds out what he is? But the spy's face is showing the complete opposite.

"How lucky you are to have someone like your

43

mother who took you in as her own," he says in a matter-of-fact way.

Antonio is astounded. He's never considered himself lucky or looked at his life in that way before.

"Life is a gift, no matter how we come into this world, kid," Chris says.

Antonio is thrown by the spy's kind words. He feels a warm feeling wash over him.

But Chris obviously has no idea the effect his words are having on Antonio. "Since you're an artist, could you gather information for me?" he asks. "Sketch and map your town – the major roads, the streets, the landmarks, the topography of the coastline and inland, nearby villages. Perhaps even document the artillery bases and track enemy movement. You'll be carrying on my observation operation in a way. And while I didn't end up in the location I was assigned to investigate, every little bit will help."

For the first time in his life Antonio sees a chance to prove his worth. A chance to choose his own place in the world – to be more than just a boy to be despised or pitied.

"Why?" Antonio says. "Are we going to be invaded by the Allies?"

The spy shakes his head. "To be honest, I don't know, kid. I wouldn't rule it out. Can you do it? Can you be a spy?"

Antonio stands and moves toward the entrance of the cave. "Let's find out," he says.

la piazza
THE PIAZZA

Over the next few days Antonio does the same thing each day. Observe. Draw. Move on. Observe. Draw. Move on. He slips in and out of shadowy corners and archways of buildings. He stands against doorways, fountains and walls that lead up steep stone stairways. He even sketches and takes notes as he snakes and winds through market shoppers and churchgoers in the piazza.

In every spying moment Antonio is nervous, excited and skittish. But he is no closer to knowing who might be *partigiani*, or part of the Resistance. He is also aware that he is racing against the clock. It's only a matter of time before another boat patrol will scour the coastline – and discover the spy.

But for today Antonio is watching people in the Piazza Salvatore, the main square of his town. He is standing in the shadows in a narrow alley that runs off the piazza. The square is buzzing with movement and the sunlight is bouncing off the crumbling facades of the buildings that encircle the piazza. The buildings are as white and decorative as a wedding cake.

Diagonally opposite, a group of old men are talking outside Pasticceria Antica. Antonio knows most of them. Signor Barbagallo, who always seems to be chewing something. Signor Portia, always smiling. There's Signor Greco, hands constantly waving and gesturing. And Signor Ensabella, always dressed immaculately.

A German soldier brushes past them and enters the pastry shop. Antonio imagines what the man will order – almond-paste biscotti! Antonio licks his lips.

Buying anything from the pastry shop is nothing but a dream for Antonio. The store's cakes and biscuits are only for the wealthy in town or the German troops, who have a serious appetite for marzipan.

Antonio thinks of Mamma Nina saying, "Antica's cannoli are said to be the very best in all of Sicily. Even the nuns don't know how to make them that delicious. I'd love to taste one once in my lifetime. But we starve while others dine on sweets. The world is absurd. Who can understand it?"

Antonio quickly sketches the exterior of the shop and scribbles the Nazi swastika beside it. He makes a note to tell the American, "Where there is sugar, there are Germans."

In the opposite corner of the square several women are gathered around local fishermen. The men are carrying buckets of leftovers from their early morning catch – the fish they couldn't sell to customers down at the beach. Antonio looks for Mamma Nina's friend Signor Piccolo, but then remembers he has left town for a couple of weeks to visit his sister in Siracusa.

But what if he's not really visiting his sister? Antonio thinks. What if it's all a cover-up? Could he be part of the underground movement?

Antonio looks at the women. Maybe one of them is a *partigiana*? Maybe the stocky one pushing the others to get her hands on the squid? Or maybe that woman standing in a balcony window watching her two small sons kicking a soccer ball in the center of the piazza? No one would ever suspect a mother. Antonio sighs. Finding the Resistance was going to be tough.

"What are you drawing?" Antonio whips round, almost dropping his notebook. It's Simonetta.

"What do you think you're doing sneaking up on me like that?"

"Ha!" Simonetta laughs. "Did I frighten you? A tough guy like you who breaks into people's homes."

"Shhh! Keep your voice down," Antonio says, snapping his book shut. "What are you doing here?"

"I'm with my grandfather," she says, pointing to the group of old men. "He wanted to introduce me to his friends and show me around town. So how is the mysterious patient feeling? Better? Did you figure out how to bandage the wound?"

"What?" says Antonio, acting as if he doesn't know what she's talking about.

"You know," she says. "The person who needed first aid."

Antonio shakes his head and begins to walk away from Simonetta.

She follows him. "You're lucky I didn't blow your cover that night," she says. "So . . . you're welcome. A thank you would be nice."

"Thanks," Antonio says, sidestepping the two young boys playing soccer. "Now, leave me alone."

But before Antonio can take another step, Simonetta snatches the notebook out of his hand

and darts across the piazza toward the group of old men.

Antonio gasps and runs after her.

Simonetta is weaving around people in the piazza. Antonio can't catch her and he's seething with frustration. She's giggling as if it's a big game.

"Give it back!" he says. But he doesn't want to make too much of a scene and draw any attention.

"Simonetta!" a gruff voice bellows. Simonetta stops and quickly flips through the pages of the notebook. Antonio twists her around and grabs it back. One of the old men is glaring their way – it's Simonetta's grandfather. "Come here, now!"

"*Si, Nonno*," she says, reluctantly walking over to him. As she moves away, she looks back over her shoulder and says to Antonio, "You're a really good drawer."

"What do you think you're doing?" Simonetta's grandfather is scolding her. "That's not how a young lady should behave. You shouldn't be hanging around grubby boys, especially him. He's a *rota*."

Antonio feels a sharp stabbing pain in his stomach. There it is again – judgment. Antonio imagines what it would be like to tell Simonetta's grandfather to go stick it.

His thoughts are interrupted by the sound of a jeep

beeping at him. Antonio quickly jumps out of the way. These days only military vehicles are allowed in the piazza. As the jeep moves on past him he catches sight of a field radio on the front passenger seat. It's encased in an olive leather canvas case – the size of a rucksack. Antonio has often seen German soldiers carrying and using them, but he's never gotten close enough for a proper look at one.

The American needs to get in touch with his contacts, he thinks. For that he'll need a radio transmitter. Antonio wonders how hard it would be to steal one. He shakes his head. How could I do that without being caught? I'd need some sort of distraction . . .

The jeep comes to a halt in the front of the pastry shop. And as if on cue, a group of Italian soldiers enters the piazza. Antonio recognizes the two men he met in the boat outside the cave, Morelli and Vitti.

He remembers part of their conversation, and has an audacious idea . . .

il gioco
THE GAME

As Antonio makes his way toward Morelli and Vitti, he wedges his notebook into the back of his pants and shoves his charcoal pencils in his pocket.

"*Ciao, amici!* Hey, friends!" he calls out cheekily, flagging their attention. "Imagine seeing you again!"

"What do *you* want?" Morelli sneers.

"Nothing," says Antonio. "But I was just thinking about how you said that Italy is better than Germany in soccer. Apparently that's not true – not according to those two." Antonio points at the German soldier, who has hopped out of the jeep and is chatting with his comrade in front of the pastry shop.

"What? What are you talking about?" says Vitti.

"They told me that our team is so weak that any German could outplay us."

"*Questo è assurdo!* That's absurd!" Morelli snorts, spitting on the ground. "Someone should remind them that we were champions in two World Cups."

"Hey, I'm just passing on what they told me."

Antonio leaves the Italians and heads back toward the German soldiers. This bit is going to be a bit harder, he thinks. He hardly speaks any German.

"Hey! *Sie sagen* . . . um, *Deutsche nicht spielen Fussball* . . ." Antonio stutters, pointing back toward the Italian soldiers, "um, *nicht gut!*"

"I speak Italian, boy, what are you trying to say?" says one of the German soldiers.

Antonio switches back to Italian.

"I just thought you might want to know that those soldiers over there – they're talking about how crazy you are for thinking you're better than them," he says. "And they said you need reminding that the German team will never be world champions. That title will always belong to Italy."

"They said that?"

Antonio nods.

The soldier translates for his friend. "Well, I've got something to say to them," he says in Italian.

The two Germans brush past Antonio and walk

toward Morelli and Vitti.

Antonio grins. They've taken the bait. He backs toward the German jeep and the radio just waiting to be stolen.

But then it gets even better . . .

One German soldier grabs the soccer ball from the two boys playing in the center of the piazza.

"Give it back!" they yell, but the soldiers ignore them.

"Hey!" the other soldier calls out to the Italians. "So you think you're better than us? *Viva Italia*? Never! No way!"

Antonio can't believe his luck. Surely Morelli and Vitti can't ignore a challenge like that.

The soldiers put down their weapons, unbuckle their artillery belts, and roll up their sleeves. Everyone in the piazza stops what they're doing and gathers around the perimeter of the square to watch the two-on-two soccer showdown.

The rules are loose, but straightforward. "First to three goals wins," Morelli announces, as more locals stream into the town square, laughing and chatting. More German soldiers come out of the Pasticceria Antica to watch and more Italian soldiers gather together forming an unofficial cheer squad. They begin to chant . . . *"I-ta-li-a! I-ta-li-a! I-ta-li-a!"*

Antonio's face lights up. No one has played a game of soccer in the piazza since the Germans moved in.

The fishermen place their buckets at either end of the piazza to serve as goals. The Germans are the first to kick off. Everyone cheers and the contest is under way.

Antonio knows he has to act fast now. He melts back into the excited crowd, and now almost everyone is cheering for Morelli and Vitti.

"Italia! Italia! Italia!"

A roar erupts as Vitti kicks the first goal.

Antonio weaves through the crowd toward the jeep. When he reaches it he takes a sweeping look around him. Good, all eyes appear to be on the game. He steps slowly back toward the front passenger seat and takes a deep breath. All he needs to do now is reach out and grab the radio. But then he spots Simonetta about twenty meters away.

She's not watching the game. She's staring right at him.

Why can't she just mind her own business? She's so annoying! Antonio thinks. He gestures to her to stop staring. Simonetta makes a face and disappears into the crowd. The crowd roars again. Another goal to the Italians.

"This game will be over soon. It's now or never,"

Antonio tells himself. The radio is sitting on the seat, just waiting for him to pick it up. He edges forward, but just as he is about to lean into the jeep, he hears Simonetta's voice.

"Hey!" she calls. Antonio freezes. He looks up to see Simonetta running toward him.

When she reaches him, she hugs him as if they're long-lost friends. Antonio tenses up. It's so strange to be held.

"What are you doing?" he hisses, trying to step back.

She whispers into his ear, "There's another soldier. Behind you. He just came into the piazza and is looking in this direction." Simonetta releases her embrace and she smiles. "You still haven't told me your name."

"It's Antonio."

"Well, that's another 'thank you' you owe me, Antonio."

Before he can say anything else, Simonetta runs off toward the German soldier.

"Help me! A thief has snatched an officer's gun belt!" she says frantically, taking the man by the arm and turning him around so he can't see Antonio. "I saw him go this way! Please! Please!"

This time Antonio wastes no time. He grabs the field radio and charges off down a narrow alley.

la pressione
THE PRESSURE

"These are great, kid!" says Chris, shoving bread into his mouth while flipping through Antonio's drawings.

"I added comments beside each landmark. And you can see I drew some maps too," Antonio tells him. "I marked out where the Germans mainly hang out in town . . . and where their bunkers are positioned along the beach."

"And what's that? In the bag?" Chris asks.

Antonio has been waiting for this moment all night and morning. He's so excited by how Chris might react that he got no sleep the night before.

"I think you're really going to like this," he says,

pulling out the field radio. "I nicked it from the Germans and now you'll be able to make contact with your –"

"No! No!" says Chris when he sees the radio. "Oh, kid, what have you done?"

Antonio is confused. He can't tell if Chris is angry or upset. "You don't like it?"

Chris sighs. "It's not about whether or not I like it. You're risking enough already. Stealing from German soldiers puts your life in peril."

"I'm sorry . . ." Antonio says, startled by the unexpected reaction.

Chris sighs heavily. "No, I'm the one who should be sorry, kid. You've done nothing wrong. I shouldn't have involved you in the first place. I didn't think enough about the fact that I'm putting a child in danger."

Antonio tries not to show how furious this makes him. "I'm not a child!" he snaps. "I'm almost thirteen! You asked for help and I can help. You said yourself you needed a radio. Well, here it is!"

Chris expression relaxes a little. "You've got a lot of gumption, kid, I'll give you that," he says. Then he smiles warmly at Antonio. "You did get a radio – although a German radio is set on a different frequency from an Allied radio. Only the Resistance will be able to get hold of one of those. But you didn't know that. I'm going stir-crazy in here – the pressure is starting to get to me. Today some patrol boats came so close I could hear the soldiers' voices. I thought I was a goner. I might not be so lucky next time."

Antonio looks at Chris's wounded leg. He's still limping and it doesn't look strong enough to tackle the steep path up il Diavolo. He wonders how Chris is sleeping on the damp rock at the back of the grotto.

"What you need is a new hideout," Antonio says. "And I've got the perfect place in mind – that's if I'm still allowed to help you?"

Chris smiles again and nods.

—

It's late afternoon and Antonio is itching to get away, but Mamma Nina needs him to help write a letter.

"Can't we do this later?" he says, feeling impatient. "The sun will be setting soon and I've got some serious fishing to do." Antonio would normally never lie to Mamma Nina, but this is not a normal situation.

"The fish can wait," says Mamma Nina. "And besides, you've returned empty-handed so many times in the last week I'm starting to think you're not meant to be a fisherman. Concentrate more on shoe shining instead. It's easy money. Signora Lari told me just the other day that a soldier had stopped her and asked if she knew anyone who would polish his boots. So forget fishing, stop fidgeting, and write for me."

Mamma Nina softly cups Antonio's cheek. With surprise he notices there are tears in her eyes.

"Do you know how difficult this is for me? I'm sorry, *figlio mio*. I'm sorry you are burdened with this."

Antonio sighs and agrees to do it. His penmanship isn't very good, but Mamma Nina can't write at all, or read. Antonio left school over a year ago to look after his mamma and earn some money for the two of them doing odd jobs. But he had learned enough to be able to write out a letter.

Mamma Nina dictates to him and he scrawls each letter and word out very slowly on a page ripped from his notebook.

"My dearest sister, Angela," she says. "I have something to ask you. The most important thing I have had to ask in my life. I hope you will be able to put aside our differences . . ."

Mamma Nina pauses while Antonio tries several times to spell out the word "differences."

". . . and forget the years between us and help your only sibling, your flesh and blood. There is no other way to say this – I am not well and might not have much time left . . ."

Antonio stops writing.

"Don't look at me like that," Mamma Nina says bravely. "We both know I'm not getting any better."

"But you said you were!" Antonio snaps, not wanting to hear it. "You are! You hardly coughed at all last night."

"Please, Antonio, just keep writing," Mamma Nina says in a frustrated and helpless tone. "Tell her this: I feel I might not have much more life in me. So if . . ." She stops and corrects herself, "*when* the good Lord takes me, I hope you will find it in your heart to make a home for my child, Antonio."

"No way!" Antonio protests. "There's no way I'm living with your sister. You haven't talked to her in years. I don't even know her!"

"She's my only living relative and, God willing, you will live with her and her husband in the house I grew up in." Mamma Nina points at the painting on the wall of her childhood home. "Or would you rather go and live with the nuns at the orphanage? Where you'll be nothing but a castoff, doing backbreaking work with no freedom to do anything else? That's no life for a boy."

"Why not? It's where I belong!" Antonio yells. "That's what people have been telling me all my life."

He knows his sadness and confusion is quickly turning into anger but he doesn't care.

"Maybe it would've been better if you hadn't taken me in . . . or if I hadn't been born at all. That's what the entire town believes – I'm nothing but a *rota*!"

"Now you take that back!" Mamma Nina says, raising her voice. "And stop feeling sorry for yourself!"

"Why? Because my feelings don't matter? *I* don't matter?"

"Of course you matter," Mamma Nina exclaims. "God brought you into this world – and we deal with whatever we are dealt. But I'm your mother and you will do as you're told."

"But you're not my mother, are you? Not really."

Mamma Nina clutches her chest and winces. All the yelling has triggered another coughing fit.

Antonio immediately regrets it. He can't take it back, though, so he tries to cover it up. "I'm old enough to take care of myself," he declares, now standing up. "And I don't need anyone to look after me."

Antonio slams the pencil on the table, grabs his fishing pole, and storms out. Mamma Nina calls after him, but he's already running down the road.

il mare
THE SEA

When Antonio reaches the beach road, he turns left instead of right toward *il Diavolo*.

The Mediterranean horizon is dotted with colorful wooden fishing boats bobbing in the surf. Silhouettes of fishing rods flick back and forth and nets are tossed overboard. Antonio wonders what it would have been like to have been born into a family of *pescatori*. All the fishermen in the town are fishermen because it's in their blood, he thinks. It's passed on from generation to generation. Is it in *my* blood? Do I come from a long line of fishermen? Or am I the offspring of a tiler, a farmer, or even a teacher?

As he heads east and follows the road along

the coast, he thinks again of Mamma Nina and is overcome by a wave of guilt.

Why did I have to say she isn't my mother? She's the only mother I've ever known, he thinks. It was cruel to throw back at her the very thing that ignorant people have said to me my entire life. Fear and frustration can make you say some stupid things sometimes. For the first time he realizes just how afraid he is of losing her.

Antonio walks at a fast pace toward Signor Piccolo's house. He stops and looks back over his shoulder to check that no one is following him. In Sicily you can always count on someone's eyes watching you. He remembers Mamma Nina saying that their island has been invaded so many times over the centuries that Sicilians are wired to be suspicious of everything.

Signor Piccolo's house is only meters away from the beach, tucked away in a small cove and hidden from the road. It will hopefully be empty for a couple of weeks while he's away in Siracusa. It will make a perfect new hiding spot for Chris.

Soon Antonio is walking from the road toward the stone villa. He wonders what it would be like to be Signor Piccolo – living alone, never married. He remembers the old man saying that he was married to the stars, sand and sea, and that it was all the family he had ever needed. Antonio ponders on that thought for a moment. If he loses Mamma Nina will the stars, sand and sea of Sicily be family enough for him? His stomach tightens and he immediately puts that grim thought out of his head.

Antonio checks the windows and front door of the villa – all locked – except for the back door. He lets himself in and begins rummaging through Signor Piccolo's bedroom closet. He finds a jacket and an old weather-beaten hat and quickly puts them on. He examines himself in the wardrobe mirror. He might not look much like Signor Piccolo, but from a distance ... well, it would hopefully be good enough.

Antonio moves to the kitchen and grabs a couple of lanterns.

He steps outside. Wild fennel bushes and rows of wild prickly pear cactus plants grow against the side of the house. Antonio steps around to the front of the villa. It's only fifteen meters to a small ridge that drops to the top of the beach – and another twenty meters or so to the water's edge. He places the lanterns and his fishing line into Signor Piccolo's wooden rowboat and rolls up his sleeves.

Here comes the hard part, he thinks, as he grabs the rope that's attached to the breasthook at the bow – the pointy front end of the boat. Antonio flings the rope over his shoulder and presses it diagonally across his chest, gripping it tightly with two hands. He takes a deep breath and pulls. And pulls. And heaves. And grunts. Slowly but surely he drags the heavy wooden seacraft toward the beach.

How does an old man like Signor Piccolo do it? he wonders. Do fishermen have superstrength we don't know about?

Antonio has been in boats many times, but he's never had to launch or steer one. He stops to catch his breath when he reaches the ridge and slides the rowboat down onto the pebbled beach.

Eventually he makes it to the water's edge and wades out into the sea, about waist depth, guiding and gliding the boat with each wobbly step – his shoes and socks completely waterlogged. Tiny waves roll in around him. The sea tonight is calm and the surface of the Mediterranean is still and reflective like a mirror.

Antonio almost capsizes the boat as he pulls himself out of the water and into it. The boat rocks and sways as he turns and faces the stern. He secures the oars into the oarlocks and lets out a huge sigh of relief. Victory! Well, a small one at least.

Antonio begins to row and the boat heads toward *il Diavolo*.

Halfway through the journey the sun dips below the horizon and the town lights begin to flicker on one by one, mirroring the star-soaked sky above. Antonio drops anchor and begins to fish, or at least tries to look as if he's fishing.

He knows that on the main beach there are German soldiers looking out for anything unusual or suspicious. He drew out their positions for Chris and he's aware that he's now in direct sight of one of the bunkers. A powerful light beam sweeps across the bay. Antonio's heart is pounding so hard it feels as if it's going to beat right out of his chest. The large searchlight flashes over the waves and directly onto him.

Antonio has his back to the beach, one of the lanterns glowing by his side and his fishing pole in position. Nothing suspicious here, he tells himself, trying to stay calm. Just a local fisherman doing what fishermen do. The German guards seem to think the same thing – there are no sirens or patrol boats rushing out to apprehend him.

Antonio exhales and thirty minutes later he pulls up anchor and continues rowing further out to sea and toward the cave.

When he approaches the sea cave, Chris appears from out behind a shrub on the base of the path that leads up to the cliff. The tide is in and has completely covered the entrance to the grotto.

"I was starting to think you weren't coming," Chris says, as he limps down the path onto the rocks. He is holding onto a cloth sack – in it is the German radio Antonio has snatched.

Antonio glides up to Chris and helps him into the boat.

"You're sure this friend of your mom's isn't coming home soon?" he asks.

Antonio nods, hoping it's true. He's already paddling back toward Signor Piccolo's place. "Lie down flat on your back and keep out of sight," he says.

"Aye, aye, captain," says Chris.

As they slowly drift back into the view of the German searchlight, Antonio stops rowing and casts his fishing line.

"What are you doing?" asks Chris.

"They have me in their sights," Antonio says. "I have to look as if I'm actually fishing."

Chris chuckles quietly. "Told ya, kid. You have the makings of a great spy."

Antonio smiles but is startled by a voice coming

out of the dark.

"Signor Piccolo!"

Antonio grumbles under his breath. He pulls a tarpaulin out from under the seat and throws it over Chris. He hopes it will be enough. Another lamp is flickering in the night and it's approaching quickly.

"I thought you were going to Siracusa . . ." A fisherman sitting in a rowboat similar to Signor Piccolo's glides closer to Antonio. He trails off when he realizes that Antonio isn't who he expects to see.

"Hey, who are you?" he says aggressively. "What are you doing with Signor Piccolo's boat?"

Antonio thinks fast. "I'm working for him," he lies. "He's visiting family and said I can use his boat to make a bit of money for myself, so long as I give him a percentage from the fish I sell."

"Really?" The fisherman glares at Antonio.

Antonio does his best to look calm.

"Now I recognize you," the fisherman adds, catching a glimpse of Antonio as the searchlight pans across him. His voice is kinder now. "You're Mamma Nina's boy, aren't you?"

Antonio nods.

"The *rota*, right?" he says bluntly.

Antonio sighs. He tries not to be offended. The man seems friendly now.

"Well, you're not going to catch anything here," the fisherman adds. "You need to go further out. And next time bring some nets. You won't catch much with a pole."

"Thanks," says Antonio. "I'll do that tomorrow night."

The fisherman continues on toward the shore.

Antonio exhales.

"Smooth talking there," says Chris, sliding the tarpaulin back from his face. "I could hear your heart beating from here. I think you should stop pretending to fish and we should get going."

Antonio agrees and starts rowing back toward Signor Piccolo's place.

When they reach the beach that leads up to the villa, Antonio and Chris extinguish the lanterns. They crunch across the pebbles toward the house.

"It's out of sight of the road," Antonio says, as they step up to the front entrance.

"Nice going," Chris says, opening the door. "I can't tell you how great it's going to be sleeping in a bed. I'll sleep well tonight."

"I wouldn't count on it!" a voice snarls as the room is suddenly flooded with light.

Antonio recognizes the Italian soldier Morelli, who is pointing his gun directly at them.

la resistenza
THE RESISTANCE

Chris reaches for his gun.

"I wouldn't if I were you!" Morelli barks. "Put your hands on your head . . . both of you! NOW!"

Morelli snatches the pistol out of Chris's hip holster. The gun is still pointed at his head. "And you!" he growls to Antonio. "Do you have a knife?"

"I don't have anything on me," Antonio says, his pulse racing. "How did you . . ."

"How did I *what*? Know that you were up to no good, you dirty little *rota*?"

"Hey!" Chris snaps.

"You say one more thing and it will be your last word," Morelli hisses, drawing his gun closer to

Chris. "Are you English? Or American? It doesn't matter. Talk about catching fish – I've just caught myself a big one, a big slippery spy. I'm going to be promoted for this, that's for sure!"

He turns to Antonio again. "The Germans alerted us that a field radio had been stolen. I got to thinking that it had been you who orchestrated the soccer game, but then you were nowhere to be seen. So today, I decided to tail you. And I'm so glad I did."

Morelli takes out a flashlight and shoves Antonio and Chris outside. "Now move it!" he orders.

Antonio's mind is spinning. What will happen to us? Will we be shot when we're handed over to the Nazis? How could I have been so careless as to allow Morelli to trail me?

When they reach the road, Antonio glances at Chris. He's limping, but he looks determined. Antonio's heart beats furiously as Chris stumbles and falls to the ground.

Morelli immediately cocks his gun. "What are you doing? Get up."

Chris groans in agony. "It's my leg." He grimaces. "It's seized up on me."

"Get up!" Morelli snaps, shining his flashlight into Chris's eyes. "Or I'll shoot you here! And don't you think of doing anything stupid, rota! Help him back up."

Antonio crouches down to help Chris. He knows this must be part of a plan. But what?

Does he want me to do something? To fight or run? Antonio decides it's probably best to do nothing.

"Can't you see he's in pain?" he says to Morelli.

But Morelli doesn't react. "If you don't get up on the count of three, I will shoot." The soldier begins to count. "One!"

Chris doesn't move. Antonio tries to read his expression. He's not giving anything away.

"Two!"

Antonio's chest tightens.

Morelli looks surprised – he expected him to move. The soldier's hand tenses around the trigger.

"NO! NO! NO!" Antonio cries, throwing himself in front of Chris. "You can't shoot!"

"Get out of the way, *rota*," orders Morelli. "Or I will make sure that not only you but your mother will be arrested and . . ."

Suddenly Morelli crumples and falls, hitting the ground hard. The flashlight rolls away.

Confused, Antonio looks up to see a figure stepping out of the darkness.

il posto di controllo
THE CHECKPOINT

"Quick! Help me get him back to the house." The voice is familiar, but Antonio can't work out where he knows it from.

He reaches for the flashlight and holds it up. A woman is standing in front of them, holding a soldier's truncheon. She's wearing a bottle-green dress and her curly ginger hair is pinned under a headscarf. She collects the guns.

"Resistance?" asks Chris in Italian.

The woman nods.

They drag Morelli back to Signor Piccolo's villa and Chris ties the Italian soldier's hands and feet together.

"I heard you behind us," says Chris, "but how did you know we were here?"

The woman glances back at Antonio.

"Well," she says. "If it weren't for your young friend here I wouldn't have found you."

"Me?" Antonio says.

"Yes," adds the woman, moving to the front door and sounding out a sharp whistle. "Well, thanks to you and my daughter."

A girl appears in the doorway. She's grinning from ear to ear.

Even in the dark, Antonio can see it's Simonetta. "I can't believe it," he says, "but I should have known. You speak English. That should have been my first clue! Of course you're with the Resistance."

"No," Simonetta's mother interjects. "Simonetta is definitely not in the Resistance. And don't put any silly ideas in her head. I confronted her about why some of my husband's medical supplies had gone missing and when she finally confessed, I decided I should also make a confession."

Simonetta smiles at her mother, who is standing by the window, keeping a watchful eye on the road.

"I'm Lucia," adds Simonetta's mother. "We'd had word that an allied plane had gone down further up the coast. When Simonetta told me this morning that you had stolen a German field radio . . ."

Chris holds up the cloth sack as if to say, "It's in here."

"Well, it didn't take much to realize that the two things were connected. So I followed you . . . and ended up trailing this soldier as well. It was clear he was after you."

"*Two* people were tailing you?" Chris says, teasing Antonio. "What happened to you being invisible?"

Antonio shrugs, embarrassed. He's annoyed – so much for having the makings of a good spy. He hopes there will be another chance to redeem himself.

"Okay, our car is here. Let's go!" Lucia announces.

"What about Morelli?" Antonio asks, noticing that the Italian soldier is starting to moan and open his eyes. "Are you going to leave him here?"

"No," says Lucia. "He didn't see who I was, but he knows you two, and this might be a real problem for all of us. So our contacts will have to deal with him."

Antonio is shocked by Simonetta's mother's harsh tone. "What do you mean?" he says.

"Kid, I wouldn't . . ." Chris cuts in, as if trying to protect Antonio from hearing the worst, which only makes him realize how naive his question is. But he wants to hear the answer – does she mean they will kill him?

"He's just doing his job!" he protests. But he can't forget that Morelli has threatened to shoot them both and has threatened Mamma Nina. They can't just let him go.

Chris shakes his head. "Let them deal with it, kid," he says. "It's not your concern."

A four-door car has pulled up at the front. Chris, Antonio and Simonetta climb into the back seat. "This is my husband, Filippo," says Lucia, introducing the driver as they speed off.

Chris nods. "I'm Agent Cooper for the OSS, but call me Chris," he says. "Are you British?"

Lucia nods.

Antonio tenses and braces himself on the seat as the car starts accelerating.

"Are you okay?" Simonetta asks.

"I've never been in a car before," Antonio says, feeling breathless.

"Never?" Simonetta repeats as the adults talk among themselves.

Antonio shakes his head.

"Can you believe all this is happening?" Simonetta says.

"You're kidding, right?" Antonio says, his hands now gripping the back of the driver's seat. "It feels as if I'm in a dream . . . I don't know whether to be excited or afraid. How did your parents become, well, a part of all this?"

The adults are now silent, so Simonetta leans into Antonio and whispers.

"They met when they were medical students in Bologna. They believe our country was wrong to side with the Germans – my mum says that's why they joined the *partigiani* in the north. My father decided they would come back here, to his hometown, to help build the underground movement in the south."

Antonio shakes his head. It's hard to believe that just a few days ago he was nothing but a poor kid who'd never left his little town, who'd never even heard of the Resistance.

Simonetta puts her hand on his arm. "By the way, I'm sorry about what my *nonno* said about you in the piazza. He's just old and he's stuck in his silly ways. I don't think he realizes that it's 1943 and that he's got to move with the times. I don't care where or how you were born. I think you're amazing."

After this compliment, Antonio momentarily forgets the thrill of his first car ride.

—

The car speeds through the night and approaches the outskirts of town.

The surrounding landscape is shrouded in darkness. Antonio has walked through it many times and knows they are driving past dusty, rugged farms. Only the lights from a few houses flicker in the distance.

Filippo slows the car and pulls over to the side of the road. He tells Chris that he will need to hide in the trunk. "We have to get past the checkpoint," he explains.

"Are you sure that's a good idea?" Chris says, hopping out of the car. "Don't you think that's the first place they'll check?"

"Trust me," replies Filippo, opening the small trunk and helping Chris squeeze into it. "I know the soldier who mans the checkpoint – he's Italian. I've been through here so many times, he's stopped searching my car. He'll just wave me through as he always does."

When they reach the entrance to the main *corso* of the town, the headlights light up the one-man booth that stands there. With a sense of dread, Antonio sees that it's a German soldier who steps out and signals them to stop.

Simonetta's father gasps.

Lucia quickly turns to them in the back seat. "You two pretend to be asleep."

Simonetta closes her eyes and drops her head onto Antonio's shoulder. He can feel her silky hair against his neck – and it sends a tingly sensation down his spine. She smells like freshly squeezed oranges.

He closes his eyes as Simonetta's father winds down the window to speak to the soldier.

"Where have you come from?" the German soldier asks in Italian.

"Good evening. Agostino isn't on duty tonight?" says Filippo casually.

"I said where have you come from?" The German soldier is obviously not in the mood for small talk.

"I've just made a house call. I'm the new doctor in town," says Filippo.

"Why take the whole family?" asks the soldier.

"Oh, it wasn't just any patient," Lucia says. "Our beloved cousin was unwell. And the children wanted to see him. But as you can see they're exhausted – we really should get them home."

There is a long, tense pause before the soldier responds. "Can you please get out and open the trunk for me?"

Antonio's stomach churns. He can feel Simonetta's heart beating faster. What are they going to do now?

Has their luck run out? Has it really come down to something as simple as this? Antonio slowly opens his eyes as Simonetta's father hops out of the car.

The German soldier shines his flashlight into the back seat of the car – directly onto Antonio. He brings his face close to the window.

Antonio says a bad word under his breath. He suddenly recognizes the German – it's the young soldier who chased him to the *il Diavolo* cliff, the one who caught him drawing anti-German graffiti.

"Hey!" the young soldier says. "I know that boy!"

i burattinai
THE PUPPETEERS

"Is this boy your son?" the soldier asks.

Simonetta's parents are caught off guard. Lucia turns to look at Antonio.

"Yes, yes. He is," says Filippo slowly. "How do you know him?"

Antonio winds down his window. "*Heil Hitler!*" he says, making a face as if to say, "Fancy seeing you again!"

The soldier tells Filippo about Antonio's offensive drawings of the *Führer* and *il Duce* – and of his incredible jump off *il Diavolo*.

"I couldn't believe it," adds the soldier. "I assumed no one could survive a leap like that."

It dawns on Antonio that this unexpected reunion might help to distract the soldier from the trunk. "Well, I might not survive my father, now that you've told him. Thanks very much!" he says boldly. "You know I'm in huge trouble now, right?"

Simonetta's mother immediately realizes what Antonio is up to.

"I'm so sorry, corporal!" she says, noticing the soldier's ranking on his uniform. "We didn't know. Offensive drawings, you say? I'm outraged!"

"Son, what were you thinking?" says Filippo. "What have you got to say to Corporal . . .?"

"Schneider," says the soldier. "It's Corporal Schneider."

This time, Antonio can bring himself to apologize. "I'm sorry," he says, trying to sound sincere.

"What's going on?" groans Simonetta sleepily, pretending to wake up and getting into the act. "What's my *stupido* brother done now?"

Antonio shoots Simonetta a look. *Stupido*? Really?

"As a part of your punishment, I think you should offer to polish the corporal's boots," says Simonetta's mother.

"Okay," sighs Antonio, opening the car door.

"No, not now," says Corporal Schneider as another car pulls up behind them. "Not now. But come back tomorrow – I'll have plenty of boots for you to shine. I tried to tell him – we Germans and you Italians, we're on the same side."

"That we are, sir," says Filippo, getting back behind the wheel. "That we are."

The corporal seems to have forgotten about opening the trunk. He waves them on and directs the next car to roll up beside him.

Lucia sighs as they drive off. "That was too close for comfort."

"Did you really jump off a cliff?" Simonetta asks Antonio, as her father drives them through the back streets of town.

Antonio nods, a little embarrassed now. "I didn't want to apologize to him. And I thought he was going to shoot me."

The car pulls up alongside a small run-down theater on a little piazza. Antonio recognizes it immediately. When he was younger he'd often sneak in to watch puppet shows here. One of the side doors swings open and a beefy bald man gestures for them to step in.

Simonetta's father helps Chris out of the trunk and Lucia takes the cloth sack carrying the German field radio.

The man hurries them through the door and leads

them through a labyrinth of corridors. Another door opens onto the backstage of the theater.

As the man shakes Chris's hand, two other figures step out from the shadows of the wings. Antonio is startled.

"This is American agent Chris Cooper," Filippo tells them.

"I'm Dino," says the bald man. "And these are my brothers, Pino and Gino. We're puppeteers – and we run the best marionette theater outside of Catania and Palermo. I have a cousin who lives in America, in Brooklyn. Do you know him?"

"Is his name *Lino*?" jokes Chris.

Antonio grins, but the '*ino* brothers don't get the joke.

"No, it's Salvatore," Dino responds earnestly.

Chris chuckles. "Sorry, I don't know him."

The puppeteers usher them into a nearby storage room. Despite his good humor, Chris looks pale and leans heavily against the wall to keep his weight off his leg.

The room is packed wall-to-wall with hand-carved marionettes. The puppets are all around a meter tall, mostly knights and warriors in shining armor with metallic swords and shields. Colorful plumes adorn their helmets.

Antonio feels surrounded. Their strangely expressive glass eyes seem to stare right through him.

"There must be hundreds of them!"

"Wow!" Simonetta says. "They're magnificent!"

"You'll be staying here . . . for now," says Dino to Chris. "Until we work out your next move and fix up that leg of yours."

"Thank you," says Chris. "I need to make contact with headquarters as soon as possible."

Lucia pulls out the German radio from the cloth sack she had been carrying.

Chris smiles. "Although my friend Antonio obtained this German radio, I do need an Allied radio."

Antonio nods proudly.

"We know someone who knows someone . . ." says Dino, taking the field radio from Chris and handing it to his brother Pino. "But we will probably have to source one from the mainland or outside the country. And it will be expensive."

Chris looks at Simonetta's parents.

"We don't have that sort of money . . . not the type of money that can get you what you want and at the same time keep mouths shut," says Filippo.

"Even if you do make successful contact, you'll

need some extra cash to arrange a smooth getaway," says Lucia. "Especially with your injury. You'll no longer be able to continue on to Northern Italy and carry out your original mission. So this will be a rescue operation. We'll need all the resources we can muster to get you safely out of Sicily. At the moment, I'm not sure how we'll get our hands on that much money."

"I know what to do!" says Antonio.

Everyone turns to him – he's so excited he can barely get the words out. "I know where we can get our hands on some money . . . a lot of it! And the owner of the money is so rotten that we won't even feel bad for stealing it."

i soldi
THE MONEY

At home, early the next morning, Antonio checks on Mamma Nina. She has been coughing all night. When he returned home, they didn't speak about their argument or the unfinished letter, even though it weighed heavily on Antonio's mind.

"I'll be back as soon as possible, Mamma," Antonio whispers, leaning in to her. "Rest as much as you can today." He turns to leave, but then walks back and sits next to her on the bed. "I'm sorry about what I said to you yesterday . . . *You* are my mother. You will always be my mother. And I love you more than anything."

Mamma Nina gently touches Antonio's cheek. She seems too weak from coughing to respond.

He kisses her on the forehead and leaves.

When he reaches the entrance of the Santa Maria the tolling of the church bell is echoing and fading into the wind. The streets are deserted – as they always are very early on Sunday mornings – but Antonio isn't taking any chances. Not after allowing himself to be trailed the day before. He double-checks that no one has followed him or is peeking from around some corner. All clear.

Antonio takes a deep breath. He feels nervous but excited about his plan. It's straightforward but highly risky. He's going to steal the Viper's money. The cash that Father Dominic is holding this week. He doesn't want to think about the consequences if he's caught.

Antonio takes another breath. He glances up at Simonetta's balcony – as arranged, the bedroom doors are open. He walks into the church.

Almost immediately Father Dominic appears from behind the door that leads up to the bell tower. An elderly woman is praying the rosary in the last pew. She glances up briefly. Antonio recognizes her – it's Signora Grasso. She looks surprised to see Antonio in church, then bows her head back into her cupped hands.

"Can I help you, my son?" says Father Dominic, walking down the aisle toward him.

"Actually, I wanted to know if *you* needed any help, Father. Maybe I could ring the church bell for you today?"

"Well, I could've used you moments ago. Perhaps we can arrange for another hour. Do I know you? You look familiar . . ."

Antonio shrugs.

"Oh, yes, you're the . . ." The priest suddenly stops himself from saying what Antonio knows he is about to say. "Unless you're staying for confession, go in peace, my son. Signora Grasso, I'm ready."

She stands up and makes her way to the confessional at the back of the church. Father Dominic looks back at Antonio before stepping into the booth.

"I'm just going to pray for a bit, if that's okay," says Antonio shuffling into a pew.

Father Dominic looks at him suspiciously for a moment before saying, "Yes, yes, of course."

The priest sits down in the booth and pulls the door shut.

This couldn't be more perfect, thinks Antonio. He is already walking down the aisle toward the open door that leads to the bell tower, hoping his shoes don't squeak on the marble floor. Climbing up the spiral staircase he eyes every brick in the wall, looking for secret holes.

Where would a priest hide a sack of money? he wonders as he reaches the top.

Perhaps it's not in the bell tower. Antonio sighs heavily. The priest might have moved it to some other place in the church.

Then, out of the corner of his eye, he spots one of the long poles the altar boys use for lighting and snuffing candles. It's propped against the wall. There are no candles in the bell tower. Antonio looks up toward the bell.

Could you hide something in the bell without muffling the sound?

"I wonder . . . " He grabs the pole, shoving it inside the bell. There's nothing there, but he does see a narrow stone shelf that runs around the opening in the ceiling above the bell.

"Aha!" he exclaims, when he feels the pole hit something. "I knew it!"

Antonio jabs at the object, yanking the pole backward, and a sack drops to his feet. Breathless, he reaches for it and takes a look inside. The sack, which is more like a pillowcase, is filled with rolls and rolls of money. Antonio has never seen so much *denaro* in his life.

He can't resist. He takes a roll of cash and shoves

it in his pocket. Then he takes the drawstring from the sack, loops it through his belt buckle, and ties it tightly.

He climbs onto the bell tower ledge. "Okay, just a repeat of the last time I was here," he says under his breath. "Nice and steady now." Antonio scans the street below one more time. No one's around. "*Uno, due . . . tre!*"

Antonio leaps onto the roof of Simonetta's building and drops down onto her balcony. He steps into Simonetta's room. This time she is expecting him.

"I've been up for hours!" she says, running over to hug him. He's too surprised to hug her back. "Isn't it exciting! I'll get my parents."

While he waits for Simonetta to come back, Antonio runs through the adventure over and over again – the moment he found the money and the leap from the bell tower. He's never felt more confident. He feels invincible.

Simonetta returns in a few minutes with Lucia and Filippo.

"Here . . ." Antonio hands them the sack of money. "I think there's more than enough to get hold of an Allied field radio and get Chris out."

Simonetta's mother opens the bag, but her father

looks nervous.

"Are you absolutely sure no one will know you did this?" Filippo asks, his face strained with concern.

"If you're caught it will put us all in danger," adds Lucia. "If there's any risk, we need to know now."

Antonio shakes his head confidently. Father Dominic won't discover the money is missing immediately, and so many people come through the church on a Sunday. It could have been anyone.

For a second Antonio thinks about what could happen if the gangster discovers that he took his stash of cash. A series of awful ideas fill his mind. He's heard that gangsters cut off people's fingers, bury people alive. But quickly he pushes the gruesome thoughts away.

"I'm sure," he says. "Will you check on my mamma for me, doctor? She's not doing well today. Right now I've got something I need to do."

—

For the first time in his life, Antonio steps inside Pasticceria Antica. He's almost overwhelmed by the wonderful aromas of coffee, almonds and vanilla. But best of all is the unforgettable smell of chocolate. *Cioccolato!*

He remembers better times before the war. A day when he was eight or nine and Signora Lari shared with them a large shard of chocolate. It was a gift she had received from a traveling relative. It was sweet and melted in his mouth. A piece of dark, velvety goodness.

Even before the war, sugar had been hard to come by unless you had money, but when the war started foods like sweets and chocolates were the first items to be rationed. Antonio could never quite understand how rationing worked, except that the government was in charge of what and how much food the people should get.

Mamma Nina said it was like a mother bird portioning out the right amount of food for her chicks, so they'd all have a better chance of surviving. But in every nest there was always one greedy chick that took more than its fair share.

So how does this tiny pastry shop in a small town still manage to supply delectable sweets in the middle of a war? wonders Antonio. Is the owner of the store, Signor Golosi, the greedy chick? Who does he know that he's able to get his hands on so much sugar and butter and cocoa?

Antonio peers into the glass cabinet at the display of *dolci* on show.

There's a small wooden radio console crackling on a shelf behind the counter. Antonio taps his foot to an upbeat song playing through the speakers. "And that was Alberto Rabagliati with *Quando la Radio Canta*, When the Radio Sings," says the announcer.

"Hey! No beggars! Get out!" Signor Golosi abruptly appears from out of the back room. "I said get out!"

"I'm not a beggar," says Antonio defiantly. "I have money – plenty of it! And if you don't want my money, I'll go somewhere else."

"Show me!" Signor Golosi demands. He squints his black button-like eyes at Antonio.

They look too small for his plump flushed face, thinks Antonio. He's looking forward to forcing Signor Golosi to be polite, to making him treat him like a customer.

Antonio waves the cash, and the storeowner stares suspiciously but only for a moment.

"What do you want?" he asks, his eyes on the roll of money.

Antonio grins. He feels special – he has a sense of power he's never had before. So this is what it feels like when cold hard cash does your talking for you. He scans the cabinet slowly, making sure he chooses the most delicious of treats.

"I'll have a couple of *paste di mandorla al pistacchio*,

almond and pistachio biscuits, four of the *palline all'arancia*, sweet candy-orange balls, three of the *casateddi* – the chocolate and hazelnut filled ones, a couple of the fig cookies and . . ."

Antonio walks over to the most-prized pastry in the store: the cannoli. Crispy fried dough rolls filled with sweet ricotta cream dotted with scrumptious chips of candied orange peel, pistachio, chocolate and cinnamon – the ones that Mamma Nina has always talked about. Once she told him that they were said to be ten times better than the cannoli the nuns from the monastery and convent made. "The nuns have the angels on their side," she said, "and they still cannot make cannoli as heavenly as the ones Pasticceria Antica makes."

"I'll have a half dozen cannoli," Antonio says.

When Antonio steps out of the pasticceria with his mouthwatering selection neatly wrapped in a flat box covered in brown paper, he feels on top of the world.

He smiles as he swaggers across the piazza, humming the song from the radio.

Suddenly a hand tightly grips Antonio's shoulder and he almost drops his prize.

"There you are, you rotten little sinner!"

It's Father Dominic.

la diagnosi
THE DIAGNOSIS

"Where is it?" the priest snaps. His expression is stone-faced and terrifying.

Antonio shrugs. "Where's what?" he says.

"Don't play dumb with me," Father Dominic hisses. "You know what I'm talking about." The priest digs his fingers deeper into Antonio's shoulder.

"Sorry, Father, I have no idea what you're talking about," Antonio says. Then he winces from the pain. "You're hurting me, Father!"

The priest releases his grip as two women walk by.

"I know you took the money, you dirty little *rota*," he snarls. "How else do you explain buying all this pastry?"

"Boot shining for the Germans," Antonio says, remembering that he still needs to do that for Corporal Schneider. "A lot of boots equals a lot of cannoli."

But the priest steps closer to Antonio and puts his arm around his shoulders.

To everyone else in the square it must look as if we're having a friendly chat, thinks Antonio.

But the priest's tone is far from friendly. "You are playing with fire, boy," he says. "If I find out for certain that you did take the money, I won't be responsible for what happens to you."

Antonio takes a deep breath. The threat is clear. He knows that Father Dominic is referring to his connection to the Viper – and what he might do to the person who took his cash. But Antonio can't in any way show him that he understands. He can't reveal to Father Dominic, not even the slightest hint, that he was the thief – not if he values his life.

So he tries to seem oblivious. "Please, Father, I really don't know what you're talking about. I swear to the Lord!"

Mamma Nina would be furious if she caught him in a lie like that, but Antonio can see he's at least put some doubt into the priest's mind.

Antonio says a hurried goodbye. He feels the

priest's stare drilling into his back until he's left the piazza and is completely out of sight.

When Antonio gets home he finds Simonetta's father looking after Mamma Nina.

"Sorry I wasn't here to meet you," says Antonio, "I was . . . held up."

Filippo looks grim. He closes up his medical bag.

"We need to talk, Antonio," he says, leading him out of Mamma Nina's room and closing the door. "The diagnosis is not good . . . Your mother is very, very ill. I'm afraid her lungs won't hold out much longer."

Antonio's chest tightens and he feels tears behind his eyes. But he's determined not to show it, not to cry.

"The thing is . . ." Simonetta's father adds, "I don't know how much longer she has. At best a few weeks, a couple of months . . . it's hard to say. But what I do know is that she cares for you very much. She asked me to help with a letter to her sister – you'll go to her and she will take care of you. I've also agreed to manage the sale of this place when she passes. You will receive the money."

Antonio's eyes begin to sting and he feels his cheeks flush.

"No! No! No!" he says. "Please don't send that letter. I don't want to live with my aunt. I don't want to live on a farm in the middle of nowhere. What sort of doctor are you if you can't make someone better?"

Filippo just places his hand on Antonio's shoulder. "I know it's not what you want to hear. But the right thing to do now is to honor your mother's wishes and make her as comfortable as possible. Look after her, lay low for the next week or so," he says calmly. "By then we might get a response from your aunt and we might know our next move with our American friend. I'm sorry I couldn't do anything more for her."

When Filippo leaves, Antonio slumps in the chair at the kitchen table. He drops his head into his palms.

One minute I'm invincible, he thinks, the next I feel like I have no control over anything.

He hears Mamma Nina stir. She calls out to him. "*Figlio*, son!"

Antonio grabs the package from the pastry shop, walks into her room and sits on the edge of her bed.

"*Figlio mio*, my child," she says. "You didn't have to call the doctor. I don't know how you . . ."

"Shhh, it's okay, Mamma," Antonio says. "I've got a little surprise for you."

Antonio helps her sit up and places the box of sweets and cannoli on her lap. He can already smell the sugar and chocolate. She pulls away the paper.

"What? From Pasticceria Antica?" she gasps. "How

could you afford this? Where did you . . ."

"Let's just say God played a part in it." Antonio smiles. "You deserve something special, Mamma."

Mamma Nina's eyes light up. It's the first time in ages that Antonio has seen her smile like this.

"Let's eat them together," she says, her hands trembling as she picks up two of the cannoli and passes one to Antonio. "After the count of three . . . *uno, due, tre!*"

Crunch goes the delicate fried pastry dough.

"Mmmm," they say together as the sweet creamy ricotta-and-chocolate-chip filling melts in their mouths.

"Thank you," Mamma Nina whispers, a tear rolling down her cheek. She embraces Antonio, pressing her face against his. "I love you, my child, I love you more than any mother can love a son."

la trasmissione
THE TRANSMISSION

A stream of excited children and parents flow into the foyer of the puppet theater. Antonio runs down the side of the building to the stage door.

He knocks three times.

The door swings open and Dino greets him. He's dressed in black from head to toe – his puppeteer's outfit.

"This way," he says, ushering Antonio backstage. He gestures for Antonio to climb a ladder that leads up to the attic.

"You're not coming?" asks Antonio, stepping up the first couple of rungs.

"No, we have a show to do," Dino says.

Antonio sees Dino's brothers – Gino is setting up the puppets and sets, and Pino is holding the German field radio under his arm. They're also dressed in black.

On the other side of the curtain the rowdy audience talks as they take their seats in the theater.

When Antonio steps up into the attic he sees Chris, Simonetta and Lucia huddled around a small radio lodged in an old leather case. Filippo is standing on a ladder looping the long aerial from the radio onto the crossbeams in the ceiling.

"Just in time, kid. We're just waiting for the valves to warm up," says Chris, also dressed in a puppeteer's outfit. He plugs headphones into the radio.

"Wow! So that's an Allied radio?" Antonio says, impressed. "What type is it?"

"This is the Paraset – made in Britain. The Allies have been dropping them to field agents in France and Belgium, but not in Italy," Simonetta's mother says proudly. "That's why it took a little time, money and effort to get it down here."

"Incredible, right?" says Simonetta. "We did it!" She slaps Antonio's shoulder.

Antonio nods and nudges her back.

"Okay, here goes," says Chris, placing a small square object into the face of the radio and tapping on a knob attached to a small lever.

"What's that?" Antonio asks.

"It's the Morse key," says Chris. "I've just sent my call signal. The key is a switching device to send out a coded signal. And before that I put a crystal transmitter into its socket."

Even though he's speaking Italian, Antonio can't make any sense of his explanation.

Chris taps at the knob again. "Nothing," he says. "Let's try this one." He reaches for another transmitter.

A few minutes later Chris makes contact – a series of on and off clicks, tones and lights come from the radio.

"Yes!" Chris taps away in response.

"I'm just giving them my status . . . in code."

Chris grabs a pencil and prepares to write down the incoming message on a blank sheet of paper. As soon as the response starts pinging on the transmitter he starts scribbling.

"They're using a cryptologic system," he says, quickly drawing up a table with columns, and placing letters and numbers in boxes.

Everyone watches intently. Antonio is impressed by Chris's skill at decoding.

"It's a double transposition using a passage from a children's novel as a key generator . . ." Chris says as he continues scrawling and unscrambling letters and figures. "I know the book and I know the passage well. It's a single quote that they're using. It's my daughter's favorite – I've read it so many times to her that I'd know it by heart even if it wasn't part of my training."

Chris ends his transmission and takes off his headphones.

"So did you crack the code?" asks Antonio. "What do we do next?"

"I know that I need to get to Catania, to the 'base of the elephant.' But I'm not sure what that means."

"I suspect it's a reference to the *Fontana dell'elefante* – that's a fountain with a Roman statue of an elephant in the Piazza del Duomo in Catania," Filippo says.

"Good. For a moment I thought I had miscoded." Chris sighs. "I'll be met by an agent there and I'll get my next instructions. They're trying to arrange for a rescue somewhere inland."

In all the excitement, Antonio suddenly realizes that he will soon have to say goodbye to Chris. His stomach churns and he is hit with a wave of melancholy. Soon he will slip back into his old life. No more adventure, no more sense of hope.

"We can leave in the morning for Siracusa. From

there we'll catch the train to Catania," says Lucia.

"*We*?" asks Chris. "You don't think I should travel alone?"

Filippo shakes his head. "Traveling with a family makes it easier to slip by unnoticed. Lucia will act as your wife and Simonetta will be your daughter."

"Hi, *Papa!*" Simonetta grins at Chris.

"Well, kid," Chris says, turning to Antonio. "It looks as if this is where we have to part ways . . ."

Before Chris can finish, Dino bursts into the room and cuts him off.

"The Germans are coming! Pino just overheard them on the field radio."

"Pino understands German?" Antonio asks.

"Of course, and it's a good thing he does," says Dino. "Because they've detected the Allied radio and pinpointed its frequency. They're on their way. But at least we have a warning, a heads-up before they get here."

"Way to go, kid," Chris says, winking at Antonio. "Stealing that field radio was genius."

Antonio grins proudly.

"Get into positions!" Dino orders.

"Positions?" says Antonio and looks to Simonetta for an explanation.

"There was always a chance this might happen

once Chris started sending out his call. The Germans are skilled at tracing radio transmissions," she says.

She's so cool and calm, Antonio thinks. It's as if she's been a spy her entire life.

"Dino and his brothers staged a puppet show at the same time so we could blend in with the audience if we needed to."

Dino starts hurrying everyone over to the ladder.

"You're part of our family," she says. "And Chris will join the brothers as one of the puppeteers."

As they run down the corridor along the wings of the theater, Antonio looks back over his shoulder at Chris. He's still limping, but Filippo has stitched his wound and rebandaged it and he looks much better. He gives Antonio a thumbs-up before he disappears with Dino in the opposite direction.

Antonio wonders if this is the last time he'll see the American.

Antonio, Simonetta and her parents slip through a side door into the stalls and move into the back row. The puppet show has already started. The marionettes, medieval knights, jiggle from side to side on the stage. The puppeteers' arms hang over the elaborately painted set, their faces hidden in the shadows above.

Antonio wonders which one is Chris. He thinks he

can guess. One of the puppets is not quite in sync with the others. The *carretto siciliano* – a colorful donkey-drawn cart – is struggling. The donkey marionette doesn't look as if it's trotting; it appears to be flying.

Antonio tries not to laugh.

He glances over at Simonetta and she smiles back. Even though he knows that they're in a very dangerous situation and they're all playacting, he feels a strong connection, almost as if he's a real part of their family. He tries not to think about it too much and turns his attention back to the performance.

Two of the marionette knights break out into an animated sword fight. As the audience cheers them on, Antonio spots an object in the back of the donkey's cart. It's the Paraset radio, but it looks just like another piece of luggage.

Talk about hiding something right out in the open, he thinks.

But just then the doors to the theater burst open and a dozen German soldiers come storming in.

la notte
THE NIGHT

"HALT! HALT!" shout the soldiers as they march down the aisles.

The audience starts booing and hissing.

Someone shouts: "What's going on? You're frightening the children!"

Two of the soldiers march up on stage. They point their guns at the puppeteers, who are still holding the marionettes, and order them to step out in front of the set.

Antonio's heart is racing.

As they line up, Chris looks cool and calm and so do Dino and his brothers.

The audience is ordered not to move.

"What's the meaning of this?" asks Dino.

"Where is it?" says the German soldier in charge.

Pino shrugs. "Where's what?"

Some of the soldiers disappear backstage. It's obvious they are searching for something. They return minutes later and shake their heads.

The soldier signals for the others to raise their weapons and point them at the puppeteers. They cock the hammers on their guns.

Everyone gasps. Many of the parents cover the eyes of their children.

Antonio turns to Simonetta's parents. "They're going to kill them," he whispers. "We've got to do something."

But Simonetta's father just shakes his head.

"There's nothing he can do without putting our lives at risk too," whispers Simonetta. "You have to stay quiet."

Antonio wants to holler at the top of his lungs, but he doesn't because just then, out of nowhere, the sounds of air-raid sirens rattle the walls of the theater. They have never been bombed before, but Mamma Nina had always said it was a possibility.

Could it really be happening? Antonio wonders. Will his town be bombed to smithereens?

Children scream and everyone begins scrambling

out of their seats, despite the guns pointed in their direction.

The soldiers look to the officer in charge for instructions, but he has already bolted from the stage and is running toward the exit.

Antonio sees Chris and the puppeteers making a run for it. Everyone is rushing to get to a cellar or a cave or hide in any type of makeshift bomb shelter as fast as they can.

They find Chris at the front of the theater.

"We dodged a bullet, but now have to dodge a bomb," Chris exclaims.

"We have a *caverna*, a cellar, at our house," says Lucia. "But we have to go now or we won't make it!"

"Mamma Nina!" Antonio says. "She's too weak to get to a shelter. I need to go back and help her."

Antonio runs a few steps in the opposite direction, then stops.

He turns back and runs to Chris. "If I . . . If I don't see you again . . ." Antonio stammers, not sure how to say goodbye.

"Thank you, kid," Chris says, holding out his hand to shake. "I will never forget you. If you ever get to America, make sure to look me up. I know my family would love to meet you."

Antonio takes the American's hand, but then throws his arms around him and hugs him tightly.

"Let's GO!" Lucia says.

"Be safe," Simonetta calls back to Antonio.

Antonio nods.

Then she's chasing after her parents and Chris.

Antonio turns and bolts for home.

"Mamma! Mamma!" he cries, charging into her bedroom.

She is under the bedcovers. "Mamma! Wake up! We have to get out of here!"

Mamma Nina groans. She seems more feeble and pale than ever.

Antonio lightly brushes the back of his hand across his mother's forehead. The sirens continue to howl across town.

"We have to go and find cover, Mamma," Antonio pleads, even though he knows it's hopeless. She is barely able to open her eyes or speak, let alone go in search of a shelter. This is the weakest he's ever seen her. She's not going anywhere.

I can't leave her on her own, he thinks. If we're bombed, then so be it. God will have to take us together, he decides.

He hops under the covers, curls up and wraps his arms around her.

She murmurs, her mouth curling to a smile.

"It's all right, Mamma," Antonio whispers, his eyes welling with tears. "I'm here. I'm here with you."

—

When Antonio opens his eyes again, after an uneasy sleep, he finds himself in complete darkness.

Outside there is total silence. No more sirens, and no bombs. This time, at least, the bombs have fallen somewhere else.

He's alive. But he knows that his mother is not.

—

Now, hours later, Antonio feels that there are no more tears left. And he's struck by what it means to be truly alone and overcome by a deep sorrow. He's in shock. He is numb. He is grief-stricken.

Antonio softly kisses Mamma Nina on the cheek, pulls the sheet over her, and with a burning ache in his heart he leaves, closing the bedroom door behind him.

He grabs his notebook and pencil and steps out into the cool night air. He runs down to the end of his lane, turns right and stops at Signora Lari's house.

He writes her a message about Mamma Nina, rips the page out of his notebook, and slides it under her door. When she wakes up in the morning he knows she will take care of what needs to be done.

When Antonio reaches Simonetta's house, he throws pebbles at her balcony window. He waits but there's no answer. He throws some more until the balcony doors swing open. It's Filippo. He gestures that he'll be down.

When he steps out, his elderly parents are standing behind him at the door, looking worried. He asks them to go back inside. They reluctantly close the door.

"What are you doing here?" Filippo whispers, standing with Antonio on the dark street.

"My mother is dead," Antonio says bluntly.

Filippo immediately embraces him. "I'm so sorry," he says. "Take comfort in knowing that she is resting in peace now . . . and no longer in pain."

Antonio's bottom lip begins to quiver. He feels another wave of tears coming, but he forces himself to stop. He has to compose himself. He is there for a reason – to see the spy – and to ask him a very important question.

"I need to talk to Chris," he says, stepping back.

"They've gone," Filippo says. "That was a close

shave at the theater and with the threat of being bombed, it was best for them to leave as soon as possible. They'll be in Siracusa by now. They'll stay there and catch the first train to Catania in the morning . . ."

Filippo stops abruptly, his gaze suddenly shifting toward the church, up to the bell tower.

A kerosene lantern is swinging, flickering in the night.

Antonio looks up and sees, illuminated by the lantern's glow, Father Dominic's face glaring down at them.

Antonio grumbles under his breath. As if this wasn't already the worst night of his life.

"What's going on?" Filippo hisses through gritted teeth, dragging Antonio inside the front door of his building and out of sight of the priest. "What has happened? What haven't you told me?"

Antonio explains everything – about the money he took to buy pastries, and about meeting Father Dominic in the square.

Filippo shakes his head.

"I'm sorry." Antonio sighs. "He can't prove it was me – he only suspects."

"Oh, he knows!" snaps Filippo angrily. "And when that gangster gets here, he'll know too. He's not going to be concerned about proof – because he'll just pummel the proof out of us. Now he knows I'm involved as well. You've put us all in grave danger by flashing that money around town."

"But . . . but . . ." Antonio stutters. He doesn't know what to say. Once again he feels like the boy he was before he met Chris – just a no-good worthless *rota*.

"Right. This is what we have to do." Filippo's voice cracks with panic and urgency. "You have to get yourself to Siracusa, quickly. Find the others before they board the train for Catania and pass this message to my wife: *Farfalla*! Butterfly. She will know what it means."

"But can't we go together? Now?" Antonio interjects.

"No, we can't. I have to make sure my parents are safe," Filippo responds gruffly. "If I can. And once you've given my wife the message, you have no other choice but to make your own way to your aunt – hopefully she will have received your mother's letter by now. Wait here . . ."

Simonetta's father ducks inside and returns moments later. He stuffs a wad of money into Antonio's hand.

"You'll need this to reach your aunt's place," he adds. "It's the only safe place now. You can never

117

come back here again. Now go!"

"I'm sorry," Antonio mutters again, before he turns, and runs. And runs. And runs. Until he discovers a bicycle leaning against a wall.

It will have to do. He knows there's no way he can reach the others in time by foot.

He hops on the bike and starts pedaling as fast as he can. Once he turns onto the road leading out of town, he picks up his pace, crunches hard on the pedals and rides into the night toward Siracusa.

l'elefante
THE ELEPHANT

It's early morning by the time Antonio reaches Siracusa. He is exhausted. His legs are sore and numb – his back is stiff and rigid.

He has been to Siracusa before, on a school trip to visit the Greek ruins. They had seen buildings that were three thousand years old. Signor Piccolo had told him it was once the largest and most beautiful city in the ancient world. But this time Antonio rides through the town at dawn. The grand piazzas and medieval lanes that lead to the sea are almost empty. The city is only just waking up.

He has ridden all night, stopping to hide on the side of the road whenever a car or military jeep drove past.

119

When he finally leans the bike against the railway station and steps into the entrance hall, he hurries to buy his ticket. Siracusa is a hive of activity. More trains than Antonio has ever seen . . . more platforms, more tracks. His town has only one rickety track and one old run-down platform – and a very small station house that is more like an oversized ticket booth.

The train to Catania is steaming at the platform, pushing out gray and white smoke in huge clouds. It's about to leave.

Antonio walks toward it but stops when he sees two figures entering the station. To his horror, he recognizes Father Dominic and the Viper.

Antonio's mind is spinning and his heart feels as if it's going to beat right out of his chest. How do they know to come here? Have they gotten to Filippo? For a moment he's terribly afraid, then adrenaline kicks in and Antonio picks up his pace, making sure to keep his back to the men.

He reaches the platform just as the stationmaster blows his whistle to signal that the locomotive is about to depart.

Antonio steals one last glance at the sinister pair – and gasps. The priest and the gangster have spotted him!

Antonio bolts toward the train, which has just

begun to rattle and chug forward. The Viper and the priest give chase. Antonio shifts into full sprint and reaches the end car just as the train is about to pull out of the station.

He jiggles frantically with the handle of the car door, before it eventually swings open and he leaps onto the train. Once inside, Antonio slides down a window and looks back to see the Viper and the priest on the platform, shrinking into the distance as the train steams ahead.

Antonio exhales. He is buzzing from head to toe, feeling exhilarated and terrified at the same time. That was close – too close for comfort! He takes a deep breath and wipes the sweat off his face with the back of his hand.

He begins to move from car to car, looking into each compartment. No sign of Chris, Simonetta, or her mother – only annoyed looks from other passengers. For a moment he worries he is on the wrong train, but when he reaches the very first car there they are, looking up, bewildered to see him.

"What are you doing here?" Simonetta squeals, jumping up and hugging him.

"How did you get here?" asks Lucia.

"Are you all right?" says Chris.

Antonio nods, stepping into the compartment.

He sits down beside Simonetta, opposite her mother and Chris.

"Really? You sure?" Chris looks at him with a concerned expression.

Antonio feels as if the spy can see right through him. He tries not to show his feelings and does his best to appear tough. But he is overcome by tiredness and emotion and is so happy to see them again that his eyes start to well up with tears.

"My mother died last night," he whimpers. "So I got on a bike and rode all the way here."

Lucia shifts across to Antonio and puts her arms around him.

"I'm so sorry, kid," says Chris. "But why come here?"

Antonio freezes. How is he going to tell them about the gangster? About the priest? Doing that will mean admitting he's messed everything up and put them all in danger. Then Chris would look at him with disappointment – the way that others have looked at him his whole life. And Simonetta will finally see that he's worthless – not amazing at all. But he has to pass on Filippo's message.

"Kid, I realize this is devastating for you," Chris adds. "But what's really going on here? You can tell me."

Antonio shakes his head. "I just wanted to be with you all. I helped you get this far, so I have a right to be here, don't I?"

Chris and Lucia look at each other.

"He can come back with us," Lucia says softly, the tone in her voice suggesting it's the best solution for now.

"Tickets, please!" announces the inspector.

When the inspector opens the door to their compartment, Lucia hands him the tickets. While he's checking them, the inspector tells them that bombs were dropped over Palermo and Marsala the night before.

"How many have died? Hundreds? Thousands?" asks Lucia.

The inspector shrugs. "No one knows yet how many lives have been lost," he says.

Chris and Lucia speculate about what this means. Are the Allies increasing the frequency of their attacks? Does it mean an invasion is coming?

Antonio listens intently but still doesn't pass on Filippo's message to Lucia and doesn't ask the question he is desperate to ask Chris.

When they reach Catania, everyone is relieved that they haven't had any direct encounters with the military, German or Italian.

"So far, so good," Lucia says to Chris as they make their way out of the busy train station and onto the city streets.

Antonio feels overwhelmed by Catania. It's much bigger, grimier, and livelier than Siracusa.

He tries to take it all in – imposing *palazzi*, wide boulevards, ornate buildings and breathtaking cathedrals. Everything is built with black volcanic stone and bright-white limestone. They walk through the crowds in the direction of the Piazza del Duomo. Antonio has never seen so many people.

"So this is it," says Chris. "The meeting point. And there's the elephant."

Antonio follows Chris's gaze.

Standing in the center of the piazza is a fountain with a sculpture of a black stone elephant on top. The elephant is smiling and on its back is a tall, white stone spire.

"*Fontana dell'Elefante*," says Lucia as they cross the square. "The locals call it *Liotru*. It's carved out of the rock that forms when lava cools. Mt. Etna is Italy's largest volcano and it's just outside town."

"That's fantastic!" says Antonio, trying to imagine what it would be like to live beside an active volcano.

But Chris is not interested in the local monuments or volcanos. "Okay, a couple of minutes," he says, looking at his wristwatch and sitting on the steps of the elephant fountain. "Everyone get into place."

Simonetta and her mother leave Antonio and Chris and wander over to take a look at the nearby church.

"Are you sure you don't want me to go with them?" Antonio whispers, sitting next to Chris.

"No," he replies. "As far as appearances go, mother and daughter have gone to pray, and you and I, father and son, are having a rest."

Chris takes off his boot and shakes it as if he is trying to get a pebble out.

"That's the signal for your contact?" Antonio asks. "So he knows it's you, right?"

Chris nods.

Antonio looks around the square. There are people everywhere – and he wonders which one of them is the agent. He looks back at Chris and tries to imagine him back at home with his wife and daughter.

"What was the book?" Antonio asks. "Back at the puppet theater when you radioed your people . . . you said that you used a children's book to unscramble a coded message."

Chris smiles. "Good memory," he says. "It's a book called *The Little Prince*. It's about a pilot who crashes into a desert and a boy – that's the little prince – who discovers him. An adventure begins and together they learn about each other and about life." Chris pauses and laughs. "Huh! Beginning to sound a little familiar, isn't it?"

Antonio also smiles, but then notices an Italian soldier heading directly toward them.

l'agente
THE AGENT

"Do you have a light?" the Italian soldier says.

"No. Sorry," says Chris.

Antonio worries that Chris's accent will give him away. His Italian is good, but he sounds nothing like the locals.

"You sure?" the soldier says, sounding surprised. "You don't smoke?"

Antonio feels his heart beating faster. It's obvious that this soldier suspects something.

Chris shakes his head.

"Hmm," says the soldier. "You look like someone who smokes all the time."

That's an odd thing to say, thinks Antonio, but

Chris looks relieved. "How many? One hundred a day?" he answers.

"Two hundred!" the soldier responds.

Chris laughs.

Antonio suddenly realizes that the Italian soldier *is* the agent.

"I thought I had the wrong man," says the soldier. "Because of the boy. Can we trust him?"

"Yes," says Chris. "If it weren't for this kid, I wouldn't be here."

The two men talk quietly, and Antonio takes out his notebook to draw the square and the elephant fountain. After a while, Antonio notices that the men look worried.

"What's wrong?" Antonio cuts in.

"The Germans have taken over a secret airfield where I was to be picked up. We're not sure if they know something or if it was just dumb luck. And now we have to find another location, one where a plane can land and get me out of here."

Something suddenly dawns on Antonio.

"What about a field? On a farm?" he says. "Would that be a good location?"

"That would work," the agent says. "If it's a relatively flat open field, then, yes."

"What about this?" Antonio adds, flipping through

the first few pages of his notebook. "It's a field on my aunt's farm, near the town of Agira."

He rips out a page and hands it to the agent. On the page is a copy Antonio had made of the painting of Mamma Nina's childhood home, surrounded by fields of sheep.

Chris and the agent agree that this could be an alternative pickup point if Antonio can find it on a map. The soldier pulls out a map of Sicily – and they pinpoint the location of the farm. As he does, two women approach the fountain and the soldier pretends he's telling Antonio and Chris how to get to the port of Catania.

"If we act fast I can arrange for a plane from Malta, most likely a Lysander," says the agent.

"I've heard a lot of good things about them – astonishingly short takeoff and landing capacity," Chris replies.

"The risk is high, but coming off a full moon, the weather conditions and light will work in our favor. I'll ask for clearance to proceed," the agent adds. He looks a little nervous because a German motorcycle patrol has ridden into the piazza. "Make sure you're on that field at zero two hundred tomorrow."

"How do I get there?" asks Chris, keeping an eye on the German soldiers as they park their motorcycles and make their way to a café.

"Can't help you there," says the agent. "But I'm sure you'll work something out. Goodbye, and good luck." The agent straightens his helmet, casually brushes the dust off his pants, and walks away.

"We're going now?" asks Antonio. "*Together?*"

"Yes," says Chris. "It's a perfect plan. You'll stay on, and I just might get out of here alive."

—

"So what's next? All good?" asks Lucia when she and Simonetta return.

Chris relays the conversation to her and explains that Antonio will now be coming with him.

"Well, then I guess this is where we part," she says. "We'll be on the next train home."

"I'm sorry," says Antonio quietly. The guilt is almost too much. He can hardly say the words, but he knows he has to. "You can't go back. I should've told you earlier, but if I weren't so stupid it would never have happened..."

"Calm down," Simonetta says. "What are you talking about?"

Antonio tells them everything and finally passes on Filippo's message to Lucia. "It's too dangerous for you to go home," he says.

"He said *Farfalla*?" Lucia says, taken aback.

Antonio nods.

"Then we have no time to waste," Lucia says in an urgent tone. "We must leave now."

"What does this mean for us?" asks Simonetta. For the first time she sounds afraid.

"I'll explain," Lucia says. "But not now."

"You've done so much for me. Is there anything I can do to help?" asks Chris.

"No. We wish you and the boy luck."

"You too," Chris adds.

"Antonio?" says Simonetta.

But Antonio feels so guilt-ridden he can't even look her in the face. He just looks down at his shoes. She's the only girl he's ever really liked and he's certain that she'll hate him forever. He doesn't even respond as he hears Simonetta and her mother walking away.

Antonio sighs heavily. So what if she *does* hate me, he thinks. I can't just let her go without telling her how I feel.

"Simonetta!" he shouts, mustering up more courage than it took to jump off the cliff. "Wait!"

Antonio chases after them.

He's breathless when he reaches her. "I'm going to miss you," he says. "Because I've never met anyone like you. At first it was because no one has ever told me I'm amazing before. You make me feel . . ."

Antonio catches his breath, overcome with emotion.

"You make me feel . . ." he stutters, "better than anyone has ever made me feel. You make me feel like I'm worth something – and that I could do anything I wanted to. But the truth is, you're the amazing one, who can do anything. And I'll miss you so much. I'm so sorry that I've put your family in danger."

"We're going to be okay," she says softly. "And you're going to be okay – you've got to believe that. I will miss you too, *stupido*."

Simonetta steps in closer, leans in, and gently kisses Antonio on the cheek.

He is stunned. He can't move or speak.

"Simonetta!" Lucia presses. "*Andiamo!* Let's go!"

"I'll never forget you," Antonio says, as Simonetta runs to her mother.

She waves back to Antonio one more time before she and her mother disappear down one of the side streets off the piazza.

il caos
THE CHAOS

"We'll head back toward the markets," Chris says as he and Antonio walk down an alley. "And see if we can hitch a ride with one of the farmers heading out of town tonight."

"My notebook!" Antonio exclaims, patting his pants pocket. "I left it on the steps of the statue. I'll be right back!"

Antonio sprints through the piazza to the base of the elephant statue, but as he scoops up his notebook the jarring wail of an air-raid siren sounds across the city. People begin to flee, crisscrossing the piazza and running for whatever cover is nearby.

Antonio bolts back down the alley where he left

Chris. He looks around, panicked, but Chris is not there.

Before he reaches the end of the narrow street, he feels himself picked up and thrown violently to the ground. An enormous blast deafens him and it's hard to breath. He coughs and splutters, and covers his head as he's showered in broken brick and rubble.

"A bomb!" he spits. But he can't hear himself speak. His ears are ringing. He feels as if he's been run over by a tank, but he only has scratches and cuts on his arms and legs.

Antonio stumbles back to his feet, dazed and groggy. Now he can hear sickening shrieks – people injured in the blast. He steps out of the debris around him.

I've got to find Chris, he thinks. The sirens continue to howl the promise of more death and destruction. This time it seems the Allies mean business.

Antonio looks up to see a squadron of planes darkening the skies. One after another, bombs drop. Pounding explosions thunder and reverberate throughout the city.

Antonio regains his balance and begins to run again, even though everything around him seems to be happening in slow motion.

Tears stream down his face as he runs around a

wailing woman hunched over her small child. He keeps moving, past men dragging bloodied people out from under collapsed buildings and military vehicles racing through intersections. Everyone is covered in ash and dust.

Finally it's too much. Antonio falls to his knees and drops his face into his palms. He is traumatized and disorientated and doesn't know what to do next. And then . . . he looks up to see a motorcycle coming directly at him through the chaos.

Antonio recognizes it as one of the German motorcycles. But *this* rider is not in uniform. Antonio jumps to his feet. He can't believe it. It's Chris!

"Quick! Get ON!"

Antonio flings his leg over the bike, holds on tight, and they speed away.

Chris twists hard on the throttle and accelerates. They zoom through the streets of Catania as bombs drop. They narrowly miss being hit by falling debris and avoid colliding with people scrambling for their lives.

Antonio struggles to stay on the bike. "Do you know where you're going?" he shouts.

"No!" Chris cries back, as he bends into another turn. "But it might not matter now, kid. It looks like we've hit a dead end, literally."

A couple of hundred meters ahead, the road is completely blocked by a collapsed wall.

"Now what are we going to do?" Antonio cries.

"Just hold on!" Chris accelerates toward the pile of wreckage. He lines the front wheel of the bike up with a long plank of wood that is lying against the rubble. Antonio knows exactly what Chris has in mind.

He holds his breath as the American revs the motorcycle, accelerates, then roars up the plank of wood that serves as a makeshift ramp.

Antonio closes his eyes as the wheels leave the ground.

The boy and the spy hit the ground on the other side of the barrier, the wheels burning rubber on the landing. And remarkably, they continue on, speeding down the road.

il pastore
THE SHEPHERD

Chris props the motorcycle against an orange tree and limps over to lean against it.

Antonio stretches and looks around. They are on a narrow dirt road surrounded by farmland and orange groves – and there's not a soul in sight. On the horizon is Mt. Etna. It stands over three thousand meters tall and its snowcapped peaks contrast against the deep-purple and blue of its wide base.

It's beautiful. The skies are clear and crisp – and the bombers have gone. Antonio can't believe that earlier in the day he was caught up in terror and now he's standing in this peaceful place.

He brushes the dust from his face and torn clothes,

and winces at his stinging and bloodied scraped legs.

"You know..." says Chris, snapping an orange from one of the tree's low-hanging branches. "In a strange way we were lucky. If it weren't for the bombing we wouldn't have had a clear run on the main roads like we did. All the military personnel were running for cover or in combat so all of the checkpoints along the way were open. I hate to say it, but the bombing turned out to be a blessing in disguise."

The American pulls out an army knife from his back pocket, slices the orange in half, and sucks the juice from it. Antonio can't believe what Chris is saying and how flippant he is being.

He's so furious that he feels as though his blood is boiling, like the fiery lava bubbling in Mt. Etna.

"A blessing?" he erupts. "How can killing innocent people be a blessing? They were just randomly dropping bombs everywhere!"

Chris remains cool. He offers Antonio the other half of the orange.

Antonio refuses angrily.

"Kid, I'm sorry," Chris says softly. "Bad choice of words. You're right to be feeling the way you are . . . but I'm not going to deny that in this case we drew the long straw."

Antonio shakes his head. "Don't you care? What

about Simonetta? And her mother? Do you think they got out of it alive?"

"Honestly, I don't know," he says. "But we can't change the outcome, either way. We can only hope they did. Look . . . over there."

Antonio turns to see, in the day's last rays of sunlight, a hillside town in the distance. "Agira?" he asks, even though he recognizes it from Mamma Nina's painting.

Chris nods. "So we must be close to your aunt's home." He pulls a map from the breast pocket of his jacket.

"Someone's coming," Antonio says.

An old man shepherding his small flock of sheep approaches them.

"*Vi siete smarriti?*" he asks. "Are you lost?"

"No, well, sort of," says Antonio. "I'm looking for Angela Cicero. I'm her nephew and I know she lives near here."

"Angela?" the old man says, waving a long stick to keep his sheep in line. "You mean Franco's wife?"

"Ah, yes. I guess . . ." replies Antonio, glancing over at Chris, whose expression seems to be telling him to stop talking.

The man looks closely at them. "That's a German motorcycle, but you're Italian. And you sound more

Sicilian than my sheep! Where have you come from?"

"Can you tell us where Angela lives?" Chris says. He hops on the motorcycle and gestures for Antonio to jump on.

"You're facing the wrong direction," says the old man. "You need to turn back and when you reach the first intersection you turn right and go for about a mile. You'll see the Ciceros' house on a little hill to the left. Are you from up north? I can't place your accent . . . are you Tuscan?"

Chris revs the throttle and pretends not to hear the old shepherd. And Antonio waves goodbye as they speed off.

"I'm sorry," says Antonio as Chris speeds on down the road. "I was trying to help. You don't think he'll make trouble for us, do you?"

Chris doesn't answer. A few minutes later he rolls to a stop at the dirt driveway leading up the hill to Aunt Angela's house and starts scoping out the surrounding fields.

It's strange to see the actual house – Antonio has known it as a painting all his life – and now here it is, real and solid in front of him. It looks as if it hasn't changed since Mamma Nina was a child.

"That's it," Antonio says, his stomach churning. "I can't believe we made it."

"Okay, this is what's going to happen," Chris declares, sounding very official and distant. "You walk up to the house, you knock on the door, and your new life begins . . ."

"But –"

"Just listen!" Chris snaps. "It will be dark soon. I'll dump the bike and make my way across these fields to that clump of woodland to the right of the house. I'll hide out there until the plane arrives. I can't risk meeting your aunt and her husband – that would put us all in danger."

"But . . . but . . ." Antonio stammers. Time is running out. "The truth is . . . I don't want to live with my aunt."

"Well, what's the alternative?" says Chris. "You can't live on your own, and you can't go back to your hometown with that gangster after you. Sometimes, kid, when change is forced upon us there's nothing we can do but to go with it. I'm sure once you've settled in with your aunt, it will begin to feel like home."

"But there is another option," Antonio says, taking in a deep breath. He has to ask now or he'll never get a chance. "Can't I come with you? Back to America. It makes perfect sense. Can I? Can I come with you?"

Chris sighs heavily.

Antonio's hopeful feeling disappears. He knows immediately that he's going nowhere. His mouth is dry. His stomach is in knots.

"Kid." Chris sighs again. "I'm sorry, but I can't take you with me – it's just not possible. But when this war is over . . . maybe, someday when you're grown up. Maybe one day you'll travel to America . . . "

Antonio turns away from Chris and begins marching toward the house. Tears stream down his dusty face. He doesn't look back at the spy.

"Hey, kid!" Chris calls out to him. "I'll never forget what you did for me!"

But Antonio doesn't respond. He just continues walking.

la zia
THE AUNT

Antonio takes a deep breath, wipes away his tears, and knocks on the door of his aunt's stone cottage.

No answer. He knocks again, but louder. This time the heavy wooden door slowly swings open.

The face of the woman standing in front of him is thin and narrow. Her wispy gray hair is tied back in a bun. It's obvious that this is his Aunt Angela – in her eyes Antonio can see a less cheerful version of Mamma Nina.

"Yes?" she asks, looking past Antonio to see whether he's alone.

"*Buona sera, signora,*" says Antonio, formally and nervously. "I'm Nina's son."

"Antonio?" she says under her breath. Then her eyes widen. "Are you hurt? What has happened?"

"Pardon?" says Antonio.

"Those scratches and cuts!" she says. "You look half starved. And you're filthy. Were you in an accident?"

"Oh," says Antonio. "I'm okay. But Catania isn't. It was bombed."

"Catania bombed? Dear Lord!" she says. "Then come in. You can't be wandering around in the night while those *idioti* are dropping bombs on us."

Antonio steps into the cottage. It smells of freshly baked bread. Aunt Angela moves toward the stove. "I was just to about to have my supper, before my husband returns from town," she says. "If you're hungry, you can have some."

"Yes, please," Antonio says politely, shuffling toward the table, hardly able to believe that he is actually standing in Mamma Nina's childhood home and feeling overwhelmed by the smell of food.

"Sit," she adds, her back still turned to Antonio. "If you're here, it means my sister is gone," he hears her say quietly. "Oh, Nina . . ."

As Antonio pulls up a chair, he takes his notebook out of his back pocket and places it on the table. It's pretty battered after all he's been through in the last few days.

Antonio sees that his aunt's shoulders are shaking, and he hears her sniffling. Is she crying?

Antonio doesn't know what to say. When she turns she wipes away her tears and serves up a bowl of *zuppa di ceci*, chickpea soup, with warm doughy homemade bread.

"*Mangia!*" she orders, hovering over Antonio. "I'm sorry to hear about your mother," she adds. "But we haven't spoken in many years."

Antonio hungrily slurps up the soup. It's been over a day since he last ate.

Angela sighs. "I couldn't have children," she says. "It's a cross I've had to bear in life. But you're not Nina's child, really, are you?"

"Yes, I am!" Antonio snaps defensively.

There it is . . . again, thinks Antonio. I'll never escape it.

"Not a child of her blood," says Angela. But then she says something that takes him completely by surprise. "Well, who am I to judge? God knows I've been at the receiving end of some cruel remarks for not being able to have children – treated as though I'm some leper. You may be a *rota*, but that does not mean a thing. Sometimes our family is not the one we're born into. Sometimes it's the one we choose. I'm sure my sister raised you as if you were her own."

Antonio nods. Finally, someone seems to understand.

"Of course, my husband won't agree with me, so let's not mention that," she adds. "For him it's all about blood, family and the old ways. But who doesn't think that way on this island?" She smiles at Antonio.

Antonio nods and mirrors her smile. He likes her.

"Listen," she says, pulling up a chair and gently taking Antonio's hands. "A word of warning. When I received your mother's letter I had decided that I would help you, but as for my husband – that's another story. It would take a miracle for me to convince him to take you in. If I say you're a great worker he just might be persuaded. But you will have to promise to work hard, be good and not cause any trouble."

It's a lot for Antonio to think about, but he nods in agreement.

Suddenly Angela's expression changes. From outside comes the sound of a horse and cart approaching the house.

"That's him," she says. "He's back."

il traditore
THE TRAITOR

Antonio catches his breath as his aunt's husband, Franco, swings open the front door.

His tanned, craggy face doesn't look happy to see a boy sitting in his house.

"Who's this?" he says, hanging up his hat and marching over to the table. Antonio slides back his chair and stands to greet him.

"This is Antonio, my sister's son," Aunt Angela says nervously. "Remember . . . the letter. He got caught up in the bombing in Catania today. And made his way here . . . on his own."

"He can stay, but only for two weeks," Franco cuts in, pulling up a chair and glaring at Antonio. "I'm not in the business of taking in strays. He can go and stay with the nuns."

"But he's family," says Aunt Nina. "And I thought . . ."

"He is no family of mine. Now . . . *Basta*! Enough! Where's my dinner?" Franco snaps. "Only two weeks – and while he's here . . . he works. You can set up his bedding in the barn."

Antonio notices the anguish on his aunt's face. She has no voice in this household. And once again Antonio finds himself wondering what his next move will be.

—

Later, deep in the night, Antonio lies under his blanket on a bed of hay in the barn. He has dozed in and out of sleep for a few hours. And even though he is exhausted and every muscle in his body aches, his mind is spinning. He thinks of Chris. It must be almost time. Soon the plane will come and the spy will be gone forever.

Antonio sits up and reaches for the comfort of his notebook. He looks at the torn paper where pages are missing – his drawings of the German bunkers on the beach, places where the troops gather. Information about his hometown that the spy might have some use for.

He can just see well enough in the light from the crescent moon streaming through the barn windows, to look at the drawings of everyone he cares about.

They're all gone, he thinks – Mamma Nina, Simonetta and her family, and Chris.

He sighs. What time is it? If he knew for sure, he could perhaps step outside and watch the plane approach – and at least see Chris as he flies away.

Antonio leaves the barn and creeps up to the front door of his aunt's house. He remembers a small clock sitting on the kitchen counter.

Just one look at the time – then I get out of there, he thinks. The agent at the elephant statue back in Catania had said to Chris to be ready for a zero-two hundred pickup. It must be close to two in the morning now.

Inside it's still and quiet – except for loud snoring coming from upstairs. Antonio holds his breath and tiptoes toward the kitchen, being extra careful not to bump into anything.

The clock's hands show that it's just before two.

On his way back to the front door, he hears the sound of a motor in the distance.

As he steps outside, a motorcycle tears down the

driveway toward the house. Antonio drops to the ground to avoid being spotted in the headlight.

He rolls under the horse cart – curling up into a ball and hiding behind one of the wheels.

The motorcycle pulls up just a few meters from the house and Antonio freezes. He gasps in disbelief. It's the gangster . . . the Viper! But how? How did he know to come here?

Antonio suddenly feels sick. He has the same unsettling thought he had when he saw the gangster and the priest at the Siracusa train station: the Viper has somehow gotten the information out of Filippo. Antonio grimaces. He doesn't want to know what might have happened to him.

The gangster steps up to the front door, kicks it open and enters the house.

Antonio desperately wants to help his aunt, but he knows that being caught there will only make things worse for them. He has to think of getting away. He has to make a run for it – now!

As he scrambles out from beneath the horse cart, his foot makes contact with a metal bucket. The clang is as loud as a church bell. Antonio gasps, running to hide behind a stack of hay bales.

The gangster rushes back outside. "Come out, boy! I know you're there! Did you really think I couldn't find you? It pays to have a priest watching his neighbors."

Antonio puts his hands over his mouth to stop himself crying out.

Uncle Franco's voice booms from upstairs. "What's going on?" he yells.

Antonio peers around the bales and sees the gangster step back inside the house. Moments later he hears shouting from both men, and furniture being knocked over and Aunt Angela screaming, "Please don't hurt him! We'll do what you say."

"This is it. I have no other option," Antonio wills himself, jumping to his feet. "*Uno . . . due . . . tre . . .* GO!"

And he bolts down the drive, away from the house.

l'aereo
THE PLANE

Antonio runs like he has never run before. His whole short life flashes before him – he sees the people who loved and believed in him, the only people who didn't see him as a castoff.

A couple of hundred meters down the driveway, Antonio tenses at the sound of the motorcycle revving up, followed by the terrifying roar of it bearing down on him. In that same moment he hears the buzz of a plane approaching from over the horizon.

Tears start streaming down his face. And as if things aren't frightening enough, suddenly three jeeps turn into the driveway, their headlights illuminating both him and the motorcycle behind him.

They're German military cars. Overcome by a paralyzing fear, Antonio's legs give out from underneath him and he collapses on the side of the road. He can see the armed soldiers in the open tops of the cars.

The men start firing and the *rat-a-tat-tat* of the shots cuts through the night.

With his face pressed into the dirt, Antonio hears what he thinks is the whirling sound of the Viper's motorcycle spinning out of control, swerving and crashing to the ground.

Without even slowing down, the Germans speed right past him. Antonio feels the hot *whoosh* of the exhausts and is almost overcome by the gasoline fumes.

They're after Chris – they must be. The German cars bump off the driveway and head across the fields. Antonio watches until all he can see are their lights. The old shepherd on the road must've alerted them, he thinks.

Antonio wobbles to his feet. Will Chris have time to get on the plane and take off before they get there?

Then he sees the gruesome sight of the Viper's body beside him. It's more awful than anything he's ever seen. He knows the man is dead. His face is smeared in gravel and blood.

Antonio feels numb – the horror he has seen no longer shocks him. War does not discriminate, good or bad. It destroys everyone.

Antonio looks back to the fields – shouting and gunshots echo across the valley. And then . . . There's a rhythmic, accelerating thrum of an airplane engine taking off.

"Yes! Yes!" cries Antonio. "The Germans are too late!"

Moments later the rattle of a piston-driven propeller whirs above him. The plane is almost invisible. It vanishes into the night sky.

"Goodbye, Chris," Antonio mutters softly. "I'm not going to live here and I'm not going to live in an orphanage. Now that the Viper is dead, I'm going back to where I belong – back to live with the stars, the sand and the sea."

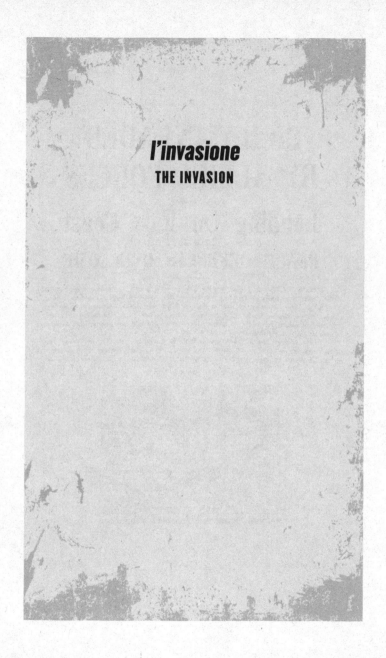

l'invasione
THE INVASION

SICILY INVADED BY ALLIED FORCES

Landing On East Coast

BEACH DEFENCES OVERCOME

LONDON, July 10.—Allied forces from North Africa, under General Eisenhower, invaded Sicily at 3 a.m. to-day. First official reports of the operation said that "everything is going according to plan."

Reuter's Algiers correspondent says that first line Allied troops attacked pillboxes and machine-gun nests along the Sicilian beaches, after negotiating mines and barbed-wire entanglements. Darkness shrouded the invasion fleet as it crept inshore. The troopships and barges and escorting warships dared minefields and strongly-placed enemy guns to reach their objective.

No information has been given about the size of the forces involved, or details of the landings. The Algiers radio says that strong air and land resistance is being met as Sicily's defences have been heavily reinforced in the last few days. The Allied invasion force includes English, American, and Canadian troops.

il ritorno
THE RETURN

Signora Lari steps out from the Santa Maria into the bright late-summer sunlight. She is elderly and bent over, but her face is round and rosy. She walks around a parked Allied Sherman tank – she's tiny next to the giant armor-plated vehicle.

As she passes a group of American soldiers, they greet her warmly and she smiles back politely – something she would never have done to a German soldier. She sees a man knocking on the door of the apartment building next to the church and approaches him.

"No one lives there anymore," she says.

"Are you sure?" he says in Italian. "I'm looking for

the people who lived here during the war – Filippo Rocca and his family – his wife Lucia, his daughter Simonetta and Filippo's parents."

"*O Dio*," says Signora Lari, making the sign of the cross. She lowers her voice. "The father, Filippo . . ." She looks back over her shoulder as if checking that no one is in earshot. "Well . . . he and his parents are no longer with us. May they rest in peace. This town escaped the bombing but we have had our share of loss."

"And his wife and the girl?" asks the man.

"I heard they fled up north. Around the same time our parish priest disappeared. There were rumors that the mother was English and a spy – you just never know about people, do you?"

The man smiles and shakes his head. "No, I guess you never do." He pauses and then says, "I'm looking for a boy by the name of Antonio. His mother was Nina."

Signora Lari sighs. "My dearest Nina. She was one of my closest friends."

"She was? So you know the boy then? Is he here?" The man frowns. "Is he . . . is he alive?"

The woman nods.

The man exhales – relieved. "Can you tell me where I can find him?"

"Oh, poor Antonio," the woman says. "I wish I could have done more for him. After Nina passed away, I wanted to take him in, but look at me, I'm an old lady, and don't have many years left, and I barely have enough to look after myself. He went to live with his aunt and uncle in the country but was not there for long."

"Yes," the man says. "I've just come from there. The boy's aunt, Signora Cicero, told me what happened, but they haven't heard from him since. Do you know where he is now?"

"He was here for a short time, about a month ago, but I haven't seen him since," she says sadly. "Signor Piccolo said he has seen him around the beachfront, and another friend of mine saw him in the piazza about a week ago. I think he just lives in the streets, like the wild child he is. Who knows where he hides and sleeps at night?"

But the man smiles.

Signora Lari notices his expression. "What is it?"

"I think I know where he spends his time," he says. "Thank you, Signora."

The man begins to walk away.

"God bless the boy," Signora Lari calls after him.

He hops into a jeep and drives through the small town toward the bay. When he reaches the beach, he convinces an American soldier to take him out on a small boat to reach the next cove.

"Over there," the man calls out, directing the soldier to steer the boat toward a sea cave, a little grotto carved into a steep cliff face. When the boat reaches the grotto, the man steps onto the rocky ledge and wades into the cave.

For a moment he allows his eyes to adjust to the darkness of the grotto and then he sees a lonely figure curled up in a blanket.

"Antonio?" he says.

The boy jumps to his feet, startled.

"Get out!" he cries. "This is my place!"

"Antonio, it's me."

"Chris?" the boy says, stepping forward until he can see the man's face. "Why are you here? *How* are you here?"

Chris takes a silver pendant out of his pocket – on it is an image of a saint and on the saint's shoulder is the baby Jesus.

"Well, your Saint Christopher medal got me safely back home, but there was something missing. Apparently there was still one more traveler he had to help," he says, handing the pendant to Antonio.

Tears begin to run down Antonio's cheeks.

"I talked to my wife about a boy I met on the other

side of the world. He needed a place where he could be part of a family, a place that he could call home, and I hadn't been able to help him. But I thought maybe we could help him now," the spy adds. "When an assignment came in for me to return to Italy, I made some calls and discovered that things hadn't worked out with your aunt . . . What do you think? Do you want to come and live with my family in America?"

Antonio rushes forward – and hugs Chris tightly.

Chris hugs him back. "I'll take that as a yes, then?" he asks.

Antonio nods.

"So, *andiamo!*" the spy says to the boy. "Let's go home."

FROM THE AUTHOR

 The setting and characters in this story are especially close to my heart. My name means "happy" in Italian and my mother was born in Sicily two years after World War II ended. My father, who is a few years older than my mum, grew up in a seaside town in the nearby southern Italian region of Calabria.

Life had become very difficult in Italy during and after the war and many Italians from these regions made the huge decision to leave. They emigrated to places like Canada, the US and Australia to seek better conditions for themselves and their families.

I've always wanted to write a novel about my parents' experience, but every time I started to write it I'd struggle. I even took my parents on a trip back to their hometowns hoping that a story would present itself. But it didn't. So I decided to let it go.

A couple of years ago, though, over dinner with my parents, the subject of "*rotas*" came up. I hadn't heard the term before and I was fascinated. It comes from the term "*ruota delgi esposti*," meaning "the wheel of the exposed children." *Rota* is an alternative spelling and I decided to go with that as I thought it would be easier for readers to pronounce.

My mum and dad were telling me about the stigma attached to being a "*rota* child" back in "the old country." Suddenly I could hear Antonio's voice, loud and clear: "Write my story!" he said. "I don't want to be invisible anymore!"

I had just finished the Andy Roid books – a series about high-tech secret agent missions – and I've always loved spy books and movies, so before I knew it, I was madly writing the story of Antonio's adventures in a world of wartime espionage.

This story is fiction, of course, but I wanted to recreate the mood of that dark period in history and at the same time present Sicily as another character in the book. I visited and talked with relatives in Italy, read stories of the Second World War and watched old newsreel clips.

If you're interested in the history behind this story, you might like to read more about it. The invasion of Sicily by the Allies was code-named "Operation Husky" and it was the first of a series of attacks on German-occupied Europe – attacks that eventually ended one of the most terrible wars in history.

But not everything happened exactly as I've written it here. For one thing, the publication of *The Little Prince* was April 1943, and I set this story in May 1943 (two months before the invasion of Sicily). Chris would have left America for training in Africa before the book was published, but it's one of my favorites and there are parallels with Antonio's story. If you get a chance, borrow *The Little Prince* from the library and see if you can figure out why I chose it.

As much as I loved writing the adventure and action in this story (and I hope you enjoyed reading it) this was always going to be more than a spy adventure. For me this story is about family and what that means. When I was a kid one of my closest friends told me he was adopted, and my first response was, "Are you going to find your real parents one day?" He explained to me that his adoptive parents *were* his real parents. Families come in different shapes and sizes – I bet you know lots of different kinds of families. Each one quite different, but each one just as important and real.

I hope you'll think of Antonio from time to time. I know

I will. And now, my mind keeps drifting to Simonetta and her mum. What did they do after the bombing? Did they still work with the Resistance? Where did they go after the war? Perhaps there's another story in that. Maybe I'll write it. Or maybe you can!

Felice

Auguri! (Best wishes!)

When Peter's family leaves for a trip across the border, he stays behind. So when the government builds a wall through the city, guarded by soldiers, tanks and ferocious dogs, he's trapped. Everyone says he might never see his family again. But Peter has a courageous plan . . .

Set in Cold War Germany, *A Great Escape* is a story of true-life heroism and the unbreakable bonds of family.

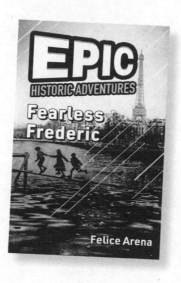

As the floodwaters rise, Paris needs a hero . . .

Frederic and his friends will have to battle an
escaped zoo animal and fight off pickpockets and
looters. But, as the danger escalates, can he find
justice for his father and discover what courage
really means?